REVAMP CAMP

REVAMP CAMP

Alice Zogg

Aventine Press

Published by Aventine Press
750 State Street #319
San Diego CA, 92101
www.aventinepress.com

ISBN: 1-59330-675-X

Library of Congress Control Number: 2010932570
Library of Congress Cataloging-in-Publication Data
Revamp Camp/ Alice Zogg
Printed in the United States of America

To Mark and Sam, my wonderful sons-in-law.

CREDITS

A special thank you to Gayle Bartos-Pool, who not only showed me her exquisite dollhouse collection but also shared and explained the craft of building miniature dollhouses, furnishings, and dolls. I can always count on Valoise Douglas to do an excellent job of editing. She has an invaluable knack for detail. When it comes to proofreading my initial manuscript, my daughter Franziska is always there for me. My gratitude goes to the members of the Los Angeles chapter of Sisters in Crime. I cherish their support and friendship. Last but not least, credit is due to my husband, Wilfried, who puts up with my absent mindedness, late dinners and forgotten obligations during the crucial time when I am in the process of plotting my story and putting it on paper.

CAST OF CHARACTERS

R. A. Huber — Private investigator; a lady sleuth par excellence

Peter Huber — R. A. Huber's husband; a writer

Andi (Antoinette LeJeune) — Huber's assistant; a dynamic young woman

James White — Owner and master of the facility; is called "The Whiz"

Doreen White — The Whiz's spouse; serves as his secretary

Doc Morrison — Camp physician; a zealous medical researcher

Heather Sotto — Matron; in charge of girls' dormitory

Kyle Norton — Sports coach; is dissatisfied with his life

Roberta Ralston — In-house teacher; uses the camp as a hideout

Bob Gilmore — Math and science teacher; lacks interest in the students

Mona — Camper; seems fearless

Tracy	Camper; is clearly frightened
Mike	Camper; a bully
Brandon	Camper; a loner
Dewayne	Camper; a street-smart young man
Jacob	Camper; a talented pianist
Tyler	Camper; has a wild imagination
Emily	Camper; has retreated into her own world
Lt. Bill Johansson	Officer of the Santa Barbara County Sheriff's Department

PROLOGUE

Faint whispering interrupted Andi's slumber, and for a moment she thought that she was dreaming. Then she became fully alert and strained to make sense of the muffled words coming from the lower bunk.

She heard a young voice murmur, "It's getting worse."

"I know," the frightened whisper came in reply.

"I think Emily is cracking up."

"I've noticed."

"We have to put a stop to it!"

"Yeah, but what can we do?"

"There is only one way out for all of us."

"You mean - -"

"Exactly, we have to kill the beast."

Andi sat bolt upright in her top bunk, holding her breath.

"Shush - - be quiet - - the new girl is stirring!"

"I'm outta here."

Then the soft sound of bare feet tiptoeing away and a moment later the creaking of a mattress on the opposite side of the dormitory could be heard before the night was engulfed in silence once again.

Chapter 1

R. A. Huber glanced at her spouse of over 40 years and asked, "What's on your mind, Peter?"

He seemed preoccupied and failed to answer.

The couple enjoyed a leisurely Sunday afternoon on the back porch of their home in Merida, located in the San Fernando Valley at the foot of the Angeles National Forest Mountains. The June gloom of the previous week had given way to early summer days of blue skies and gentle temperate breezes. The smell of freshly cut grass drifted over from their neighbor's yard. They sat opposite one another at the white painted round iron table, he in a matching patio chair and she on the old-fashioned loveseat swing, which was propped up against the house wall.

Huber took a sip from her glass of cranberry juice and studied her husband. His hair had turned completely white, and even the prominent eyebrows and mustache seemed to get lighter with every new day, but his hazel eyes were forever steady and held strength of character. I wonder if he sees me as the old lady that I've become when he looks at me, she mused. It seems only yesterday that we met and fell in love, raised Deborah and Ben while working hard to make ends meet. We've had our share of fights, but overall, life has treated us well, she reflected.

Suddenly aware of Peter's eyes searching hers inquiringly, she said, "Let's face it, we are no longer a middle-aged couple, but fast approaching old age."

"Speak for yourself!"

"Tell me the truth; do I look 'over the hill'?"

Amused, he scrutinized her from head to toe. What he saw was a good-looking face framed by salt-and-pepper hair. The laugh-lines around mouth and eyes and the slightly sagging chin reflected a life lived to the fullest. An undisputable vitality radiated from the trim athletic figure as she was swinging on the loveseat. And she managed to look chic even in her own back yard, wearing what she called her "bum" clothes and no make-up.

Peter winked and replied, "You can't be 'over the hill' as long as you kick butt on the racquet ball court, solve a few crimes, give a five-course dinner party, and keep me entertained when we turn off the lights – all in the course of a day!"

She laughed and said, "Then never mind me, but what's brewing in your head? You've been dwelling on something ever since coming back from your writer's conference." She added, "And don't try to make me believe that it has anything to do with books or literature."

"You know me so well, Regula! Actually, the problem does not concern me, but a fellow author. Do you remember my writer friend Roger Hawk?"

"Vaguely."

"He sat on the panel with me at the conference and we went out for a drink afterwards."

"Sounds reasonable, so far," she teased.

"Roger looked a nervous wreck, and after a lot of coaxing, he finally told me what was bothering him. It has to do with his teenage daughter, Emily."

"What about her?"

"Apparently, she had become too much for him and his wife to handle and they enrolled her in some facility."

"What kind of facility?"

Peter explained, "I understand it's a 'tough love' rehab outfit for juvenile delinquents, run like a boot camp."

"I've heard that some of these places have a high success rate in turning troubled kids around," his spouse commented.

"Yes, and this one came highly recommended, and although there are restrictions, Roger and his wife had great expectations that their daughter would be in good hands and that the people in charge would help her shape up."

"What restrictions?"

"For instance, the kids are not allowed to have any visitors the first two months of their stay. Not even parents are admitted on the premises."

"That makes total sense to me. People in authority at the facility can't be expected to have any kind of success with the juvenile delinquents while having parents meddle every step of the way."

Peter said, "Phone calls are monitored also. Parents may call once a month, but no other calls are permitted."

"That too seems a good policy. So what's the problem?"

"Well, now that their daughter is staying at the camp, the Hawks are getting bad vibes about the place."

"Why?"

"They cannot get in contact with Emily, and they are starting to have a creepy feeling about it."

"How long has she been there?"

"A little over a month."

She raised an eyebrow and said, "Didn't they agree to the policy of not seeing their daughter for two months when they enrolled her?"

"Yes, but evidently they have not talked to her on the phone either."

"You just told me that parents were allowed a phone call per month, and she's been there longer, right?"

"Exactly, but each time they make the call, the person in charge tells them that Emily doesn't want to talk to them."

"That *is* rather strange, unless the kid truly hates her parents."

Peter continued, "Personal belongings are not permitted, so anything like a cell phone or computer gets confiscated upon arrival. Like I said, Roger is worried that something strange is going on."

"So there is nothing he can do short of bursting into the place and taking his daughter out of the program."

"I guess he's not willing to do that, yet."

"Where is this rehab located?"

"It's a place near Solvang called Revamp Camp."

"The Danish town north of Santa Barbara?"

"Correct."

"How old is Emily?"

"Sixteen."

His wife mulled their conversation over and then asked, "Think your friend is overreacting?"

"Possibly, but maybe his fears are valid and there is something wrong at Revamp Camp. Roger wants to hire you to drive up there and investigate. I told him that they might not let you inside the camp, but he suggested that you could stake the place out and snoop around."

After a moment's reflection she stated, "I can do better than that. Don't you think Andi would make a convincing juvenile delinquent?"

Chapter 2

Antoinette LeJeune, better known as Andi, buried her father before her 18th birthday. A few months later, after having settled his estate, the young woman traveled west. She had packed a touring bag with personal essentials plus her two pieces, the Derringer and the Stinger pen pistol, mounted the inherited Harley-Davidson, and left her native New Orleans behind. Now, three years later, she had acquired an associate's degree of art from Pasadena City College and planned to transfer to UCLA in the fall to study for her bachelor's. The young woman had made new friends and a good life in her current habitat, yet was occasionally homesick for Louisiana and, above all, missed Daddy.

On Wednesday morning in early July, Andi left her kinfolk's home in Pasadena, straddled the Harley, and started on the two-and-a-half-hour journey to Solvang. Having memorized Mrs. Huber's instructions on how to get there, she was riding in the diamond lane - - happy to have that privilege as a motorcyclist - - until it ended shortly before the 134 W. freeway automatically turned into US-101 N. At that juncture, traffic got hectic for a while, demanding Andi's total concentration. Soon she was fortunate to have "easy sailing" once again and let her mind wander. She was debating whether to stay at Auntie Sue and Uncle Earl's house once she started at UCLA, or if finding a place on the West Side was the better choice. Not having to make the commute every day would be great, but could she afford an apartment in that area, even with a roommate? There was another downfall for moving near the university. She'd be far from Mrs. Huber's office in Pasadena.

With regard to her kinfolk, she had had no choice but to take them into her confidence about going to Revamp Camp. After all, she couldn't just leave without telling them her whereabouts or Auntie Sue was liable to report her missing. Andi was excited over her assignment at the camp. Granted, she had helped Mrs. Huber with many cases, but she hadn't been *on the spot* and under cover since that very first time at Optimum House in the Big Bear area. She thought, I handled myself well up there and I was only 18 then. Now I'm a lot older and have more experience; this'll be a piece of cake.

She was riding along the outskirts of Santa Barbara when she stopped her musing and paid attention to the surroundings. There were two ways of getting to her destination. She could continue on 101 and exit at the town of Buellton, or take the 25-mile mountain road out of Santa Barbara heading north. She chose the latter, never able to resist riding on curvy alpine terrain. She turned onto CA-154, leaning into each looming curve on the steep, winding uphill road. At the summit, she had a great view down to the valley and then needed to watch her speed on the descent. She passed several horse ranches before Cachuma Lake stretched far into the canyon in front of her eyes. Then she turned left into CA-246, which landed her straight on Mission Drive in the endearing small Danish town of Solvang. She smiled to herself and thought, might as well have lunch since it may be my last meal as a free person.

Solvang was founded in 1911 by three members of a group of Danish educators. The plan was to establish a Danish village, where the arts, crafts and customs of their homeland could be created anew, and to build a Danish Folk School. Enchanted by the natural beauty and ideal climate of the region, they purchased 9,000 acres of the old Spanish land grant, Rancho San Carlos de Jonata, naming the place Solvang – English translation: Sunny Meadow. The village was "discovered" by visitors in the late 1940's who gave it a year-round economic boost through tourism.

Andi did not know all this when she strolled along its streets flanked by shops and restaurants full of old-world-charm. After a fair amount of browsing and window shopping, she settled on a small restaurant with outdoor seating.

She did not bother to open the menu and asked the waitress, "What's your most popular lunch?"

"That would be smørrebrød," was the reply.

"I'll have one of those."

Before long, she was served an open sandwich consisting of a slice of buttered dark bread topped with a piece of fish that was generously garnished. The entrée tasted delicious. Thus fortified, Andi thought it was time to find Revamp Camp.

Chapter 3

Leaving the village, Andi continued along Mission Drive to the small town of Buellton less than four miles away. She rode through Buellton, and about two miles farther, there was a dirt road on the right, leading slightly uphill. This must be the way to the camp, she thought, and followed the arched lane, kicking up dust at each curve. Enjoying the twisting terrain, she continued on until she came around the last bend and arrived at her destination. Stopping her bike by the sign that read *Revamp Camp,* she planted her feet firmly on the ground and took a good look around. Straight in front of her was an iron gate and behind it, she got a glimpse of a large ranch-style structure. What impressed her most was the immense fence as far as the eye could see. I reckon this here is what people call "a fully gated community," she thought.

There was a dirt lot to the right of the entrance gate with about half a dozen parked cars. She killed the engine and eased her Harley in a space between a silver Lexus and a banged-up pickup truck, then stayed put for a couple of minutes to rehearse what she was about to tell once being admitted inside the camp walls. She briefly mulled over Mrs. Huber's instructions: "Stick to the truth as far as your

background and most everything else. The only lies you
will have to tell are your reasons for seeking out the rehab
facility." Her boss had left the details of these fabricated
reasons up to her but had warned against making them
too complicated. She had also advised her to stay clear of
anything that could be easily proven to the contrary. For
instance, Andi could not claim to have ever been arrested
or that someone had brought charges against her.

After Mrs. Huber's briefing, Andi had given the matter
a lot of thought. Posing as a kleptomaniac had come to
mind, but she soon rejected the idea since shoplifters
usually leave behind a record. As far as she knew, most
juvenile delinquents had problems with drugs, alcohol,
or both. Having never taken any illegal drugs, she
probably could not effectively fake being an addict. She
was no stranger to alcohol, though. After all, Daddy had
owned a bar in the French Quarter. So liquor it is, she had
concluded.

Yesterday, when she had called the rehab center's office,
the lady who answered had been pleasant enough. It was
established that there was space for her at the camp and
that she could enroll immediately, if she wished. Packing
her touring bag this morning, Andi heeded the woman's
warning, "Don't bring anything that could be remotely
considered a weapon. If you do, it will be confiscated." So
she was going into the wolf's den without a pistol or even
her treasured Swiss Army knife. Her boss had presented
her with the knife on her last birthday, and she had carried
it in her pocket ever since. Now she felt naked without
it. With an impish smile she thought, if I have to defend
myself, I can only use the gifts that God gave me: my body
and my wit. The woman had also instructed her to leave
personal valuables at home or the items would be taken
away.

She removed the helmet and shook her abundant auburn hair loose. Then she tucked her headgear under one arm while grabbing the touring bag and the second helmet strapped to it with her free hand. She took a deep breath, set her mind to the role of a juvenile delinquent, gave the Harley one last look, and then walked rapidly toward the gate.

Chapter 4

Doreen White sat at her computer in the spacious administrative office of Revamp Camp trying to make a dent in the workload at her fingertips, but her mind kept wandering. She was petite at five feet tall, 96 pounds, and seemed even tinier seated in the large room among massive furnishings. At 42, she was still a pretty woman with big brown eyes and dark wavy hair framing her doll face. At the moment these fawnlike eyes stared into the monitor, unseeing. No matter how hard she tried to concentrate on work, her thoughts drifted aimlessly.

She wished that her recent vacation on Maui would have invigorated and refreshed her body and spirit, but to her horror just the opposite had occurred. She felt more and more discontented with her life at the camp. She had never been able to match the zest and enthusiasm James had about the place, which remained to this day, nearly nine years after starting Revamp Camp. To him the rehab facility, and the success of it, was as important and life-sustaining as breathing in and out. Granted, he was brilliant and doing wonders with the young people in his charge, who seemed to respect and look up to him. She knew that his work was worthwhile and fulfilling, yet she had expected more out of life and their marriage when she had accepted his proposal over a decade ago.

Doreen sighed and looked out the window, trying to ignore the bars encasing it. She spied a hummingbird fluttering close to a hibiscus before it finally landed on the bright red flower, taking nourishment into its long beak. For an instant, the tiny bird hovered in her view before it flew off in a flash. She thought, I envy you your freedom, little creature. Then her mind floated back to her previous musing. She loved and admired James, but was that really enough? It would be different if they had children. He regarded the juvenile offenders as his kids and cared for them as if they were his own. It did not work out that way for her. Looking at herself honestly, she had to admit that she didn't much like the kids and was clearly afraid of some of them.

Did I just hear the noise of a motorcycle approaching? she wondered. Listening intently for a moment and not perceiving another sound, Doreen decided that she must have been mistaken und went back to her reverie. She was aware that soon her biological clock would stop ticking. Also, she was by no means sure if she even had the physical stamina to go through childbirth for the first time at this point in her life. It was certainly not too late to adopt, she decided. I must bring up the subject once more with James and convince him of my point of view, she told herself. Thus having come to a decision, she could now focus on her secretarial tasks, but before she had entered the first line on her computer the gate buzzer went off.

Chapter 5

Andi stared into the camera mounted above the gate and yelled, "Antoinette LeJeune here!"

"Please, you don't need to shout. Stand back; I'll let you in."

With a sharp clanking sound, the iron gate opened, and as soon as Andi had stepped through, it rolled to a close. Andi flinched when the gate snapped shut behind her with a final thud. She thought, I'm an inmate now.

Doreen White was waiting at the main entrance of the building and watched as Andi approached, taking long, determined strides. What she saw was a tall young woman sporting a mass of unruly waves of auburn hair and, despite the warm weather, clad in jeans, a black leather jacket and cowboy boots. She carried some sort of tote bag and two helmets.

Pointing to the second helmet, Doreen asked, "Is there someone with you?"

Without the slightest embarrassment, Andi said, "No, that's just my security blanket."

The older woman shrugged and led the way to the administrative office, saying, "As you may have guessed, I'm Doreen White and we already spoke on the phone."

Andi was pleased to find the room air-conditioned and said, "That's right."

"I understand that you are 21 and are here of your own accord."

"Yes, ma'am."

"My, my, you are quite the Southern Belle," Doreen declared with a chuckle. Then she handed her a form and said, "My husband will talk with you personally and show you around, but first we need to get you established, so have a seat and fill this out."

Andi grabbed the pen and form attached to a clipboard and settled herself in one of the armchairs scattered around the spacious office while Mrs. White went to her desk in an effort to get some work done.

The form was four pages long, and Andi dashed through the personal data like name, address, phone number, gender, age, and so forth. Then she came to a section where she needed to give her medical history as well as her mental health history. Behind the latter, the words "if any" were written in parentheses. The mental health field was the first of many that she left blank. She applied a checkmark by the word "alcohol" in the substance abuse part of the form.

When finished, she signed and dated the document and brought it over to Mrs. White, who browsed through it and then stated, "Seems all clear."

Then she said, "Now, Antoinette - -"

"Please call me Andi."

"Very well, Andi it is." And scribbling 'prefers to be called Andi' on the form, she continued, "I understand that your parents have both passed away; I'm sorry about that. Are - -" she looked down at the sheet of paper in front of her "- - your Aunt Sue and Uncle Earl responsible for paying our fee?"

"No, ma'am. I can manage it myself. Daddy left me some money."

Doreen looked up sharply and asked, "We *did* discuss the amount over the phone, correct?"

Andi's cat-like green eyes took on a mischievous sparkle as she replied, "I know it's a fortune, but I can handle it."

Then Mrs. White held out her delicate small hand and ordered, "Your wristwatch, please."

Astonished, Andi took it off and, handing it over, said, "You told me no jewelry, but come on, an ordinary watch?"

"That's considered a personal valuable. Besides, you won't need one here."

That said, she opened her desk drawer and took out a zip-lock baggie and, reaching for a black marker, labeled the plastic bag with Andi's name and the current date, and then dropped the Timex into it.

She explained, "This will go into your file, and you'll get it back on the day of your discharge. Is there anything else you're wearing or carrying that I should know about?"

"I don't think so."

"No cell phone, computer, or the like?"

"No, ma'am."

"Where's your purse?"

"I didn't bring one."

Doreen looked puzzled for a second and then said, "Oh, of course! You came on a motorcycle." And pointing to the touring bag, she asked, "Is your wallet in there?"

"No, my billfold and checkbook are in my pockets."

"Hand me both, please"

"You're jivin'!"

"I'm dead serious. Your items are a lot safer with us than they would be if we'd let you keep them. You certainly don't need any money here, and you don't need an ID on your person while at Revamp Camp; we know who you are. Should you be permitted to leave the premises during your stay, we'll hand you the items."

Andi stood up and took both things out of her front jeans pockets and then placed them reluctantly on the desk. There was only a small amount of cash in the billfold, and she had left her credit card at home. Still, she felt uneasy about handing over her ID. Also, she carried Daddy's picture in the wallet and had misgivings about it being tossed into some file.

Doreen labeled another baggie and dropped the checkbook and wallet inside.

"Wait a minute! If I stay here more than two weeks, I'll need my checkbook to pay the bills, yours included."

"You may come to the office at any time and take care of business."

Andi looked at her keenly. Was the woman making fun of her, she wondered? No, apparently Mrs. White was on the level.

"All right, you may take your seat again in the waiting area." She turned her head away from Andi and spoke into the phone, "The new camper is ready for you."

While waiting for Mr. James White to appear, Andi congratulated herself on having managed so far without telling an outright lie. It was true that she was in possession of an inheritance from Daddy, and it was also accurate that she would be writing the checks to the order of Revamp Camp. The fact that Mrs. Huber's client was footing the bill, and that the first installment into Andi's account had already been made by Roger Hawk, was just a slight omission.

Chapter 6

To Andi's surprise, it was not the leader of the camp that came to fetch her, but a tough-looking woman in her thirties, who kept her ash blond hair cut short and straight, wore jeans, a t-shirt and what looked like hiking boots.

Mrs. White made the introduction, "This is our new camper, Andi." And indicating the woman, "Meet Matron, Heather Sotto. Ms. Sotto will screen you and then show you to your assigned space in the dormitory."

Andi stood up and was at eye level with the matron, which meant their height was even at 5' 9", but Ms. Sotto was about 40 pounds heavier.

The matron looked Andi over and said, "If you follow the rules, we'll get along just fine, but if you mess with me, you'll live to regret it. Is that clear?"

"Yes, ma'am."

"Come along, then."

Andi followed her out of the office, down a corridor and up a flight of stairs. Sotto pointed to the end of the hallway and said, "Over there is the boys' dormitory and scrub room. Those quarters are off limits to you. Understood?"

Andi looked her in the eyes and was certain that the matron dared her to have a peek at the boys' quarters. She replied, "Yes, ma'am."

"And you have no business on the entire opposite wing either. Those are the rooms of Mr. and Mrs. White as well as Roberta Ralston's."

They entered something that looked like a locker room in a gym. There were showers along one wall, toilet stalls and sinks off another, a row of lockers against the third, and a large metal table in the center of the room.

Ms. Sotto said, "We're in the girls' scrub room. This is where you're going to take showers, get changed, and use the toilet." She came to a halt in the center of the place and ordered, "Put all your stuff on the table."

Andi complied, and the matron proceeded to take everything out of the touring bag. There were several pairs of pants and tops, sneakers plus a pair of flats, socks, underwear, an extra bra, and pajamas, as well as Andi's toilet articles. The matron took all the items out, examining each thoroughly before placing it on the table. She studied each object in the small makeup bag and went to the trouble of feeling along the seams of every garment. When she had taken out the last piece of clothing, she turned the empty bag inside out. Then she scrutinized the two helmets and seemed particularly intrigued with the old one.

She finally said, "You rode in on a bike?"

"Sure did; on my Harley."

"Alone?"

Andi nodded.

"So what's the relic for?"

"That was Daddy's helmet. I take it along wherever I go."

"Your father is dead?"

Andi nodded again.

After a pause the matron said, "We usually don't allow any needless items, but I'll let you keep the extra helmet. Take all your stuff except toilet articles and pajamas and put them in locker number eight."

The lockers were large and resembled mini-closets with a row of hangers and a small shelf. Andi stowed everything away in her assigned locker and closed it.

Then she turned around and said, "Where are the padlocks?"

"There aren't any. The campers don't keep valuables, so there's nothing to steal."

"Makes sense."

"Now I need you to strip."

"Pardon?"

"Take your clothes off."

"Everything?"

"Yes."

Ms. Sotto examined each piece of clothing thoroughly as Andi disrobed. She paid particular attention to the leather jacket, removing items such as goggles, gloves, and a pair of regular sunglasses from its pockets and then meticulously went through the lining, feeling for any possible bumps or irregularities. Since Andi's front jeans pockets had previously been emptied in the administrative office, only some loose Kleenex, and a chap stick was rolling out of a back pocket when the matron turned it inside out. Despite a detailed search and padding down of the cowboy boots, there was nothing to be found there, and the socks, panties and bra all passed muster.

Then the woman eased her hands into surgical gloves and said, "Spread your legs."

Andi was already embarrassed enough to have to stand around naked in front of a stranger, but what happened in the next second overwhelmed her with humiliation and anger.

She yelled, "What the hell are you lookin' for?"

"Concealed drugs, of course."

"In my vagina? Holy Krewe!"

In an instant the search was over, and the matron said, "You can get dressed now, and then I'll take you to the dorm."

The girls' dormitory was a gigantic hall with a sitting area at the entrance and to the side a cubicle with drapery drawn around it. Ms. Sotto opened part of the curtain to reveal a double-size bed, a nightstand, and a small wardrobe.

She said, "This bed is mine, and being the matron, I'm permitted some privacy."

The rest of the space was wide open and held two rows of bunk beds against the walls running parallel with the long sides of the rectangular room.

The matron indicated a billboard at the head of the room and said, "Go over the rules now so there won't be any misunderstanding."

Andi read: *Dormitory Rules*

> 1. Dormitory is off limits to campers of the opposite gender
> 2. No visiting in each other's bunks
> 3. No cussing or foul language
> 4. No running or jumping
> 5. No food or drink
> 6. No yelling; keep voices low
> 7. Lights out and silence at the 10:00 p.m. tooting of the horn

Then she walked Andi to a bed near one of the windows and stated, "The upper bunk is yours. There's a niche where you can store your toilet articles and pajamas, and if you need extra blankets, there are some in the closet at the other end of the dorm. Fresh towels and washcloths are also in the closet. Shower-gel and shampoo is directly dispensed inside the shower stalls in the scrub room."

The matron went on, "The laundry room is in a separate structure behind our building; you may use it during your free time."

Andi had taken a couple of steps over to the window and was looking out, barely listening to the other's instructions.

Ms. Sotto said, "Any questions?"

"Sure do! I can understand the reason for the bars on the windows downstairs, but why up here? I mean, we are on the second story and I'd say about 20 feet above ground level. There are stone plates on the platform directly beneath these windows and no trees close to the structure. Anyone trying to break-in, or more to the point, break-out, would be out of his mind."

"The point is," the matron replied, "we are not concerned with break-ins or -outs, but are worried about suicide attempts.

Chapter 7

Andi did not know what she had expected the master of Revamp Camp to look and act like, but she was blown away by James White when she stepped inside his small office. He was probably in his forties, but clearly hip. A vast forehead stretched above his narrow nose, and he kept his long brown hair pulled back and tied into a ponytail. He sported the rugged complexion of an outdoorsman and the charisma of an entertainer. The man's most impressive feature was his eyes, which where deep-set, steel-gray and penetrating. His handshake was firm when he stood up to greet her, and she noticed that he was wearing khaki cargo pants and loafers with no socks.

He motioned her to a chair across from his desk and, after sitting back down on his, leafed through the form in front of him, saying, "Let me quickly go over your data."

This gave Andi time to have a look around his office. It was sparingly furnished, and save for a framed black-and-white print depicting a farmer tending to his crop, there were no decorations or knick-knacks displayed of any kind. He must not spend much time in here, she thought.

He suddenly lifted his head and said in his deep, commanding voice, "So you go by Andi?"

"Yes, sir."

"Call me Whiz."

Andi stared and then asked, "Just Whiz?"

"Years ago, a grateful parent of one of my success story campers called me the 'Whiz of Rehab' and the name stuck." Then he said, "You have a bit of a Southern drawl. Where are you from?"

"New Orleans was my home, but now I live with kinfolk in Southern California."

"Sorry that your parents passed away. When was that?"

"I never knew my mama. She died when giving birth to me. Daddy went about three and a half years ago."

"Not because of Hurricane Katrina, I hope."

"No, sir - - I mean, Whiz - - he died of liver disease."

"Did your father raise you?"

"Sure did."

"Tell me a little about your upbringing."

"Daddy never remarried, so it was always just him and me. He taught me stuff, like how to play the fiddle and dance the Cajun Waltz, fishing, riding the Harley; loading, shooting and taking care of a gun. He was a dang good cook too and showed me his tricks with pots and pans."

"I see." And after a pause he said, "Your case is unusual; you are 21 and you're taking the initiative for being rehabilitated. Typically, my campers are younger and their parents bring them to us under protest."

Andi said, "So am I the first delinquent to come willingly?"

"No, it happens, but I prefer to call my charges campers."

Then he said, "You left the referral line blank. How did you learn about Revamp Camp?"

"Searched the Web under 'rehab facilities' and there you were," Andi replied.

He glanced down at the sheet of paper in front of him again and asked, "Do you consider yourself an alcoholic?"

"I'm not sure."

"What is your daily intake of alcohol?"

Andi knew that she was treading on thin ice with where the questioning was going and needed to be on her guard in order not to be exposed as an imposter.

She replied, "I don't drink every day, but when I do, I can't stop."

"And then?"

"I keep drinkin' until I pass out."

His steel-eyes held hers for what seemed like an eternity, and she had the feeling that he was looking right into her soul, but her glance did not waver.

He finally said, "What else?"

"Sometimes I don't remember what I did when drunk."

"And you hate when that happens?"

"I loathe it!" And suddenly she threw herself into the role and pleaded, "Please, Whiz, help me! I'm enrolled at UCLA and need to be cured before the fall semester starts."

"I can't guarantee that, Andi. Some people take many months, even years, before they can stand on their own two feet where alcoholism is concerned. You seem to be motivated to quit and you came here of your own accord. That is certainly a plus, but as I said, there is no warranty as to how long it will take. We'll just have to take it day by day. In worst case, you may have to postpone starting college."

He continued, "You say you don't take drugs and you don't smoke. If that proves to be the truth, we can solely concentrate on your alcohol problem."

"It *is* the truth," Andi stated.

Then he said, "I see that you're Catholic. Are you fanatical about it?"

"What do you mean?"

"Do you insist on having to attend a service at your church every Sunday? If so, I'd have to arrange for an escort, since campers are not allowed off the premises without supervision."

Andi replied, "I don't go to Mass every week."

"We provide a nondenominational service here, geared to any religion, Christian or otherwise. Everyone is welcome, but nobody is forced to attend."

"Okay by me," she assured him.

He gave her his charismatic smile and said, "Now, let me tell you a little about what we do here at Revamp Camp, besides the obvious. We grow our own produce and there are no domestic employees; the campers take care of all household chores. Everyone, staff and campers alike, chips in with the labor of tending to the crops, except for my wife, who is too fragile, and Doc Morrison, who does research in his lab when not engaged in the treatment of his patients."

Andi said, "The doc is a shrink, right?"

"Doc Morrison is our doctor and psychiatrist. He treats the campers for anything from minor physical ailments and injuries to drug abuse and mental health disorders. And like I said, in his spare time he does medical research."

Andi had been puzzled ever since arriving at the camp at how quiet the place was. With juvenile delinquents around, why wasn't there any noise? Come to think of it, she hadn't seen a single kid yet.

So she asked, "Where are your campers?"

"A handful are in the fields, but most are still in class." And he looked at his wristwatch and stated, "School will be out in a few minutes."

Of course, Andi thought, these kids would be of high school age. She was wondering what lay in store for her during the time that classes were in session.

As if reading her mind, the Whiz said, "Our schooling is year-round at high school level. Sorry, we don't provide college courses, but we'll find a way to keep you busy."

He went on, "It is important to keep physically and mentally fit, so I encourage our young people to be active with sports and hobbies. However, these are privileges that are taken away if there is any misconduct."

Andi donned her best juvenile pout and said, "I'm amazed that you allow hobbies, since we can't have any valuables or personal property." And she gave him a nasty look when she added, "After enduring the matron's frisking, I'm surprised you don't make us wear uniforms."

Unperturbed by her outburst, the Whiz remarked, "We actually used uniforms in the very beginning, but when Doc Morrison came on board, he made me see that it is important for the campers' mental health that each keep some sense of individuality."

Then he asked, "What do you like doing best, Andi?"

"Ridin' my bike."

"Oh, that's right; my wife told me that you arrived by motorcycle. What kind is it?"

Andi proudly replied, "A 1990 FXR Super Glide."

The Whiz was clearly at a loss and admitted, "I'm afraid that I don't know much about motorcycles."

"I'm talkin' vintage Harley – Davidson, and she's a beauty!"

"Of course I cannot permit you to ride your bike outside the camp, but maybe we can figure something out within our walls."

Then he got up and declared, "Come, I'll show you around."

Chapter 8

The Whiz took Andi on an expedition of the building and its surroundings, and she could tell that he enjoyed the role of a tour guide. The place had been converted from a ranch with 150 acres of land, he told her. The high school classes were held in a separate structure, remodeled from what had originally been the horse stables.

On leaving his office, he pointed toward the end of the hallway and said, "Over there is Doc Morrison's office and lab. You'll see him soon for your examination and drug testing. And on the other side of the corridor is the staff bathroom, which is off limits to campers."

Then he turned back toward the front entrance and waved to his spouse as they passed the open door of the administrative office. He showed her around the opposite side of the building and made explanatory comments as he opened each door. There was a mess hall with a large kitchen next to it, and even though the Whiz called it "our eatery," it looked like a typical mess hall to Andi. The kitchen was all stainless steel, immaculate, and devoid of people. He remarked that soon the place would be bustling with campers preparing supper. On the opposite side the kitchen opened up to a small room furnished with just a minuscule table and four chairs, and he mentioned that some of the staff, including his wife, preferred to eat their meals there.

Next, he took her to another large room, which he called the assembly hall, but failed to explain what kind of assembling he had in mind. At the head of that room there was a platform that looked like a church pulpit, and a slew of folding chairs were neatly stacked up against the length of one wall. Otherwise the place was without furniture. He showed her a hobby room that also served as a library, and there was a music chamber with a piano and several other instruments lined up against the wall.

In addition to the toilets in the scrub rooms to be found upstairs, there were also separate camper bathrooms for each gender on the ground floor. The real eye-catcher was a huge board attached to the hallway wall. It appeared to be a task chart of sorts.

Andi studied the billboard and asked, "What's this?"

"That is the schedule to show each camper what chores and duties he or she is assigned to for the week. We rotate the jobs, so the list gets changed every Monday." And he added, "Since you are joining us today, Wednesday, and have not completed your admitting process yet, you will start your duties in a few days. If Dr. Morrison is through with you by Friday, Ms. Sotto will find something for you to do for the remainder of the week. On Saturday evening, you may look for your name on the board to find out what job you are assigned to for the coming week."

Andi thought, I hope it's not latrine duty, but kept quiet.

Then the Whiz said, "You've already seen the second story, so let me show you our crops."

As they stepped outside via the back door, the blast of a horn – so loud that it could be heard for miles around – boomed three times in a row.

Startled, Andi pulled back a step and blurted, "Holy Krewe! Where's the fire?"

He gave her a reproachful stare and said, "That had better not be profanity. I do not tolerate foul language."

"No sir, a Krewe is an organization that parades at Mardi Gras."

"Is that a fact? To answer your question, the sound you heard was the signal that school is out. One toot is for getting up in the morning or for lights out at night; two is to gather for meals; three informs students that classes are either starting or ending; and four blasts is the command for all to come together in the assembly hall."

They were walking toward a structure that was obviously the school building; a steady stream of kids was emerging from it. As each teen passed by, he or she would voice a greeting like, "Hello, Whiz!" and Andi was surprised to notice the admiring glances the inmates gave him. Almost worshipping, she thought. Adjacent to the school house was a baseball field, and her guide informed her that it could easily be converted into a soccer field, if need be.

Before long, they had left the school building and sports-field behind and were striding along a path in the direction of the farmland. They walked by a tool shed with a small Kubota tractor, a tiller, as well as a cultivator parked next to it. Presently, apple orchards came into view.

The Whiz said, "As I mentioned, we grow our own organic fruits and vegetables and bring the excess crop to the farmers market in Solvang held there weekly. There is a supply of well water and the land has a subsurface mainline with aluminum irrigation piping."

Andi pointed to a bunch of trees and asked, "What kind of apples are you growing?"

"Those are Galas and they'll be ready for harvest in mid to late August." And indicating an orchard on the opposite side of the trail, he remarked, "Over there are Golden Delicious, not ready to be picked until September."

They came upon a huge garden with dozens of rows of vegetables of all kinds. The Whiz introduced his produce when they strolled by and elaborated on each species as proudly as a farmer might show off his crop. So Andi learned that lettuce took 70 to 80 days from planting to harvest and that the tomatoes were ripe now and more plants were growing to last well into September. The number of watermelon fruits per vine varied from 2 to 15, and they reached maturity approximately 45 days after blooming. She noticed that pole type green beans needed trellising, and the Whiz informed her that the pods were already full-sized and that he would give the order to start picking them tomorrow. When they passed near a row of bush peas, he commented that they were not doing well this year because the weather had turned hot too early.

A distance away, a small group of people were hunched over and crouched close to the ground and Andi asked, "What are they doing?"

"Digging up potatoes," he replied. "We planted these potatoes in January, then plowed and cultivated them. Their harvest began in May and continues all through summer."

When they got closer, the campers looked up and as if on cue, they all called out, "Hi Whiz!" He returned their greeting with a wave of his arm. Then they stooped down again and continued with their task, while the Whiz led Andi farther along the path.

Coming around a bend, they suddenly stood at the base of a good-sized vineyard stretched out over the hillside.

Amazed, Andi said, "You're growing grapes? That's awesome!"

"Yes, we do. The Chardonnay green-skinned grapes are used to make white wine, and the dark ones for Pinot Noir. Everyone at Revamp Camp will lend a hand at the grape harvest next month."

Playing up her chosen persona, she asked, "So where are you hidin' the wine cellar?"

He flashed his magnetic smile and replied, "Sorry, we don't make the wine ourselves; that would be too much of a temptation. The grapes are driven to a vinery nearby to be crushed. Then they'll sit in a barrel for several months before being bottled. I share the profit from the wine - - if there is any - - with staff and campers as a thank-you for their labor."

Andi thought, he's covering his butt so nobody can accuse him of using his inmates as free labor.

Aloud she proclaimed, "That's mighty generous of you!" Then she thought about the concept a little deeper and asked, "How do you do that since we're not allowed to have our own money?"

"Simple," he replied, "the amount is either deducted from our fee, or the camper is paid out the cash when he leaves."

Then he said, "Our goal here is healthy, clean living; no drugs, alcohol or tobacco, and plenty of exercise." He stopped walking and turned his face toward her, holding her gaze with his hypnotic stare and stated, "And any *liaison* between boy/girl - - or same sex for that matter - - is strictly forbidden. Do I make myself clear?"

"I understand the word."

He shot back at her, "I do not take kindly to attitude from my charge, and you had best drop yours!"

"Yes, sir."

Having trekked in silence some five minutes along the fruit-laden vines he said, "This pathway leads beyond the vineyard, where it curves around the western end of the property in a semi-circle and then runs along the lower wall of the estate, but it's time for us to head back."

So they turned around. The kids had left the potato patch and the farmland looked deserted. When they were even with the sports-field, they saw a middle-aged muscular man guiding one camper with blood gushing from his nose while dragging another kid by the arm.

The Whiz said, "Hey, Coach, what happened?"

"These two got into another fistfight."

"Is Dewayne hurt badly?"

"Only a bloody nose, I'd say, but I'll have Doc check him over, just in case."

"Good idea." Then he glared at the two boys and said, "Mike, I'll see you in my office on the double! And I'll deal with you, Dewayne, after Doc Morrison is through with you."

"Yes, Whiz," the kids said in unison.

Chapter 9

Andi sat in an upright chair in the waiting area in front of Doc's office, expecting to be asked inside at any moment. The Whiz's earlier words suddenly hit her: "If Dr. Morrison is through with you by Friday..." What's he going to do to me for two days, she wondered? Before she had time to dwell on it further, the door opened and the kid the Whiz had called Dewayne emerged. His nose was no longer bleeding, but a shiner below one eye had started to form. Otherwise, the teen seemed no worse for wear. He was thin with lanky long legs and seemed about an inch shorter than Andi, but judging by his enormous feet in proportion to the size of his body, she was sure that the boy was still growing. The African American kept his hair shaved close to the scalp, except for a line of curls sticking up through the center of his head in a Mohawk. He was about to pass by her with his customary swagger when Andi got up and stepped in front of him.

She said, "Hi there, I'm Andi. And I believe your name is Dewayne?"

"Uh-huh."

"Feel okay now?"

"It was only a bloody nose; no big deal." Then he looked her over and said, "You're not a camper, are you?"

"Sure am! Got here today." He eyed her skeptically, and she added, "I know I seem old to you, but I'm basically just a messed up kid like everybody else."

"What you're here for then?"

"I'm an alcoholic. How about you?"

"Drugs," he replied.

"So you're a drug addict?"

"No, never touched the stuff myself; I was dealing."

Andi couldn't think up a comment fast enough, and Dewayne dodged by sidestepping her, saying, "The Whiz is waiting for me. See you."

Moments later, Andi was facing the psychiatrist. He first ordered her to give a urine specimen. There was a small bathroom with toilet and sink inside his domain, and she was glad that she did not have to walk around the building with her transparent container of yellow fluid in hand. He explained that the other door led to his laboratory, which was absolutely off limits to everyone other than the doctor himself.

His spacious office sported a huge desk, an upholstery group, the typical psychiatrist couch, an armoire and a gigantic bookcase stacked with mostly medical science journals. All the furniture was of solid oak, with one exception. There was a straight-back chair with a sliding plastic tray mounted on top of it. It was to that chair that he directed Andi when she came back from the bathroom. She sat down, and the doctor slid the tray in position and gave her a small ball to squeeze.

When he pulled the tourniquet tight on her upper arm, she suddenly knew what was to come next and protested, "What are you takin' my blood for?"

He swabbed her with a brown liquid and, while inserting the needle into her vein, said, "I need to test you for ethanol toxicity."

"What was that brown stuff you put on my arm?"

He replied, "That was a Betadine solution; I can't very well swab you with alcohol when I'm testing your blood alcohol content."

She was mad now and said, "I didn't drink today; you won't find any. You could've just asked and saved ourselves the trouble."

"Sorry, I can't take your word for it."

It was over with quickly, and then he walked her to his desk, grabbed his chair and told her to get comfortable in hers. She sat down and faced him expectantly across the desk.

His fingers flew over the computer keyboard and, staring into the monitor, he said, "Mrs. White has already entered your info, so let's see what we've got."

Andi studied him as he concentrated on reading her personal data. He was fairly young, in his late thirties, she figured. Blue-eyed and sandy-haired with regular features, he could have been considered good-looking, if it wasn't for his ears. They were huge and stuck straight out. A button-down striped shirt was visible underneath his lab coat. She noticed that his hands were extremely white, with well-manicured nails. No tending to the crops for you, Doc, she thought.

He looked up and stated, "You are not suicidal - -that's a plus - - and if the information you provided us with proves to be correct, you are not an alcoholic in the traditional sense of the word. I suspect that you simply are obsessed with alcoholic drinks but by the same token have a low chemical tolerance to alcohol. That does not necessarily mean that your condition is easy to cure. On the contrary, it will require a lot of patience on your part. We have to get to the bottom of determining the real cause that makes you drink in excess."

Andi was not sure what kind of reaction to this news was expected of her; she just knew that she had to be careful. This shrink would see right through her if she let down her guard. So she did not say anything and just looked at him wide-eyed.

He said, "I'll go over the lab results with you tomorrow. Come and see me in the morning right after breakfast and we'll start the treatment."

That stated, he let her go.

Chapter 10

So far so good, Andi mused, lying in her upper bunk revisiting that first day at the camp in her mind. She had been accepted into the group at face value, it seemed, and if she was careful not to blow her cover, she was here to stay. Except for Dewayne, she had not had a chance to chat with any of the inmates yet. At dinner, the Whiz had introduced her by name as the new camper, but she was left in the dark about who her peers were. She had been unable to strike up a conversation with anyone during the meal, not even the kids immediately seated on either side of her. It was impossible to talk since campers were taking turns going to a lectern at the entrance of the mess hall and reading aloud from a book.

She had not paid much attention to what was being read but gathered that it was meant to be inspirational. Instead, she had focused on watching the people in the room. Some of the kids' faces indicated they were listening to the words, but most just seemed to concentrate on shoving food into their mouths. There were three rows of long tables, seating about a dozen kids and an adult at the head of each. The Whiz presided over the middle table, the coach supervised another, and she had been assigned to sit at the matron's.

The kids were not separated by gender, but rather mixed throughout the three tables. Andi guessed that there were about 35 kids at Revamp Camp, with two thirds of them being boys. Later she had counted twelve occupied bunk beds in the girls' dorm, so her estimation had been fairly accurate. The girl in the lower bunk was named Mona, but that was all she knew about her. Mona had avoided talking to her under the guise of needing to be quiet in the dormitory.

Andi continued her train of thought. Her first impression of the place was that of a well-organized rehab facility due to the strong leadership of the Whiz. The man seemed to have his campers under total control and they evidently adored him. There were strict rules to adhere to, but that was only natural for an institution like this, she deduced. So far, she could not detect anything strange going on.

I wonder which one is Emily? was the last thought she had before dropping off to sleep.

Later in the night the whispering voices of Mona and another girl awakened Andi from a deep sleep. She would have ignored the interlude and gone back to her dream world had it not been for the words she overheard, "…we have to kill the beast," at which time she sat bolt upright in her top bunk.

Sleep did not come to her again until the early hours of the morning, and shortly thereafter she was abruptly roused by the wake-up toot of the horn.

Chapter 11

In the master bedroom at the opposite wing of the building, Doreen had also had a restless night. The evening had started pleasantly enough with James being his charming self, sweet-talking her into a false sense of contentment. His lovemaking that followed had been intense and left her glowing and slightly out of breath. She was always amazed of how passionate he still was after over a decade of marriage. Now would be a good time to bring up what had been on her mind for weeks, she decided.

Before she had a chance to verbalize that thought, he said, "Mike and Dewayne were at it again today. You'd think that since neither of these boys have any substance abuse problems, they would be easier to handle, but apparently that isn't so. Dewayne will probably come around, but I'm starting to doubt that I'll ever get through to Mike. According to Doc Morrison's findings, Mike has deep-rooted problems from which he may never fully recover. I'm not surprised; having been shoved from one foster home to another ever since he was two years old must have left a permanent scar."

He sat up in bed and continued, "That boy looked me in the eye today and stated that he knew what was going on here. I wonder what he meant by that?"

Doreen started to open her mouth, but James went on, "I'm a little puzzled by Andi, the new camper. She - -"

"Will you forget about the campers for a sec!" his wife shouted in frustration. "I don't care about them! What about me? I'm totally unhappy in this place of screwed-up kids, don't you understand?"

James was speechless for a second. Then he said, "What on earth has come over you? You've always known that rehabilitating these kids is my life."

"Well, it isn't mine!"

"I thought that you'd come back from Hawaii refreshed. Didn't you have a good time there?"

"Not really. I wanted to go on a trip with *you*, not with some girlfriend. Is that too much to ask? Aside from a prolonged weekend here and there, you haven't had a proper vacation in years, for crying out loud!"

"You know good and well that I can't leave the campers unattended for any prolonged amount of time."

"Yeah, yeah, yeah!"

"What do you suggest? A divorce?"

"Of course not. I want a baby."

"Come on, Doreen, you know that we cannot bring up a child at Revamp Camp; we've discussed this before."

She had argued her point of view at length until she realized that James had stopped listening and was fast asleep. She silently cried tears of disappointment, knowing that nothing was gained and that she wouldn't get any rest all night.

Chapter 12

On Thursday morning, Andi came out of the eatery in good spirits, having consumed an excellent breakfast of pancakes. Last night's chicken dinner had been tasty too, she thought. The place may not have any domestic employees, but the kid assigned to kitchen duty was a dang good cook. There were no readings held at breakfast, so she had talked to her neighbors at the table.

Brandon, seated to her left, was a shy boy of seventeen, giving mostly yes or no answers to her attempts at conversation. She did glean that he had been at Revamp Camp for six months. On her other side sat Jacob, who told her that he was a musician, a pianist to be exact. He had chiseled features with expressive brown eyes that seemed full of sadness, and the hand that grabbed the fork to eat his pancakes was delicate, the fingers long and narrow.

What she had overheard during the night didn't seem all that menacing in broad daylight. She might have misunderstood the girls' barely audible chat. So it was in a receptive mood that she entered Doc Morrison's office.

He greeted her with, "Yesterday's tests show a blood alcohol level of far below 50 milligrams per deciliter and you are also drug free. So you're clean, Andi."

"What a surprise," she said sarcastically.

"All right.   I'm going to start you on Antabuse treatment."

"What's that?"

"It is an adverse treatment.   Antabuse is the brand name; the chemical name is disulfiram.   The medication produces sensitivity to alcohol, which results in a highly unpleasant reaction if you take in alcohol while under treatment."

"What kind of unpleasant reaction?"

"You'll get sick."

Then the doctor checked his computer screen and said, "Just making sure all the information I have on you is accurate.   You are not currently taking any kind of medication, correct?"

"That's right."

"And you are not pregnant?"

"No, sir."

"We can proceed, then."

He took a tablet out of a container, crushed it and mixed it with water, saying, "Since your weight is on the light side, I'm giving you a lower dosage than average. I'll prescribe a disulfiram 250 mg daily dosage." And handing her the glass, he added, "This medication alone will not cure you; you'll need counseling sessions as well."

The stuff had hardly any taste to it, so Andi downed it to the last drop while the doctor walked over to the big armoire and opened its doors.

Andi gasped in astonishment and blurted, "Holy Krewe! You've got a fully stacked bar in there!"

The armoire held an assortment of hard liquor, including bourbon, scotch, gin, vodka, tequila, rum, and so forth, as well as many brands of beer and wine. Mirrors mounted to the inside walls of the furniture gave the display of bottles a glamorous touch. Andi was suddenly overwhelmed by a warm and homey feeling. All those drinks lined up and nicely arranged reminded her of Daddy's bar in the French Quarter of New Orleans.

Misinterpreting her longing glance, Doc Morrison asked, "So what's your pleasure?"

"You want me to have a drink?"

"Anything you like," he replied.

"Wait a minute, I just downed that medicine. I'll get sick."

He nodded and explained, "That's part of the treatment; you need to get ill and disgusted with alcohol before you can get better. So what'll it be?"

Andi surveyed the selection and thought, my best bet is a drink with the least amount of alcohol. So she said, "I'll take a Miller Lite."

She was aware of his watchful eyes when she started to drink the brew, so she pretended eagerness. He made a show of walking back to the armoire and closing the two wing-doors, locking them, and pocketing the key.

"Just so you know, the armoire is always locked up when I'm not here, and I also lock my office door when I'm busy in the laboratory."

Then he said, "We might as well start with the discussion therapy. Tell me a little about your upbringing."

While sipping her beer, Andi started recounting her life story, similar to what she had already shared with the Whiz. She was disclosing what a mean jambalaya Daddy used to fix, when it hit her. First she experienced a throbbing in her head and neck, followed by shortness of breath, and then the nausea came on with full force.

"Excuse me," she managed to say on her sprint to the bathroom.

When she came back, exhausted and shaking, the doctor directed her to the couch and said, "Lie down, you'll be sick for some time to come."

The next few hours were a blur to Andi. She was either bent over the toilet retching, or curled up on the couch in misery. Oblivious to her surroundings and barely aware of the stream of kids coming for their sessions with the Doc and leaving again, she just wanted to lie there and die. Did she hear moaning nearby, or was she hallucinating?

She was in agony for most of the day, and to the doctor's credit, he stayed close by and monitored her vital signs every so often.

Chapter 13

On her second night at the camp Andi was stretched out on the upper bunk reflecting on the drama of the day. She had never been so sick in her entire life and was determined not to repeat the experience, no matter what booze the shrink offered her next time. But that was the whole point. Drinking alcohol while being treated with that Antabuse medication was such a bad trip, a kid would think it over hard before doing it again. Well, Doc would soon find out that she was a fast study. Does Mrs. Huber have any idea what my posing as a camper involves? she wondered.

In the late afternoon she had kept a Seven-Up down, and by evening felt well enough to try some food. When she heard the horn tooting twice, she had gathered in the mess hall with everyone else. However, as soon as she looked at the stew in her plate, she couldn't bring herself to sample a single bite. To her surprise, shy Brandon addressed her soon after she sat down. She now replayed the dialogue in her mind.

He had said, "You look a little green. Did you have Doc's shock treatment?"

"Sure did."

"Let me warn you, no matter how long you've been taking the Antabuse tablets, you'll never work up a tolerance to them. You'll always puke when drinking while on that stuff."

"Are *you* still on the Antabuse treatment?" she had asked.

"Not anymore, but I'm on MMT."

"What's that?"

"Methadone Maintenance Treatment for heroin addiction."

Andi would have liked to hear more, but the first reader went to the podium and the opportunity to talk was over.

Before lights out, she had exchanged a few words with Mona, who was 5' 2", had dark hair, brown eyes, and an attitude. Still not feeling well from her ordeal, she was sweating and had pulled her covers off. They accidentally landed on the lower bunk.

Mona had hollered, "Hey, up there, watch what you're doing!"

"Sorry."

"Just because I'm small and Philippina doesn't mean I'll take crap from anybody."

"If you're lookin' for a fight, you're outta luck, girl. I had a treatment today and am too ruined to take the bait."

A big chuckle came from the lower bunk and then Mona stated, "You're a riot!"

"Friends?"

"Maybe," came the reply and then the horn sounded and the lights went out.

Chapter 14

By midmorning on Friday, Andi left her therapy session with Doc Morrison feeling confident that she had not made any major blunder and hadn't blown her cover. The doctor first handed her the Antabuse dose and watched as she drank it. Then the psychiatric session began. He wanted to know more about her childhood, but hardly asked any questions while she babbled on about whatever entered her mind. It felt good to talk about Daddy, something she hadn't done in years. Before she knew it, the half hour was over and he dismissed her, saying, "See you on Monday."

It was true that she did not need her wristwatch while staying here; besides the tooting of the horn at different times of the day, there were big wall-clocks staring her in the face in most rooms and hallways. When she came out of the shrink's office, she had just enough time to use the restroom before having to report for kitchen duty.

A female camper was already in the kitchen standing near one of the sinks, unsure of what to do. Andi had noticed the girl in the dorm. She and Mona seemed to be close and Andi suspected that she might have been the other person whispering in the lower bunk.

The girl seemed nervous and said, "Mrs. White is gonna be here soon."

"What's your name?"

"Tracy."

"You're Mona's buddy, right?"

"Uh-huh, we're best friends."

"I'm Andi."

"I know. Are you feeling better today?"

"Sure am! That was a nasty experience I had. Are you also on Antabuse?"

"No, I don't have a drinking problem. I'm being treated for a coke habit."

Tracy was blonde, blue-eyed, and seemed afraid of her own shadow. She kept her voice low, and her eyes darted to the open door and back, as if she was afraid of being spied on. When Andi gave her an encouraging smile, the girl lighted up a little and said, "Your hair is the coolest shade of red. I've noticed it before, but it looks even better up close."

"Thank you!"

"How often do you have to touch up the roots?"

"Never."

"You're kidding; it's natural?"

"Like Daddy used to say, *le bon Dieu* gave it to me."

Tracy stared and then said, "Oh, I get it; Dieu is French for God. Is your dad French?"

"No, he was Cajun."

"Cool!"

Andi would have liked to question her about what she had overheard on the first night, but the sound of footsteps echoed from the hall and then Ms. Sotto walked in.

The matron stated in her usual abrupt manner, "Mrs. White went to Santa Barbara and left me in charge of the kitchen for the day." And stepping over to the pantry, she continued, "The teachers and Doc Morrison won't be here for lunch, so we'll keep it simple and fix peanut butter and jelly. Go wash your hands and let's get started."

They applied team-work in the true sense of the word when fixing the sandwiches. Tracy spread peanut butter on some 40 pieces of whole wheat bread, Andi smeared strawberry jelly on their counterparts, and Ms. Sotto put them together and then cut each in half. Next, Andi's job was squeezing lemons for making lemonade while Tracy sliced watermelons.

Andi had tried to converse with Tracy while on the sandwich assembly line, but the girl had been unwilling to talk ever since the matron joined them.

Getting fed up with the silence, she now asked Ms. Sotto, "Are these lemons coming from trees at Revamp Camp?"

"Naturally," she answered.

Andi did not remember having come across any citrus trees when touring the fields with the Whiz, but she probably hadn't seen half of the compound yet.

It was clear that the matron was also a woman of few words, and so the lunch preparations continued without conversation. Minutes before the sound of the lunch bell tooted, they carried trays with the fruits of their labor into the mess hall. Then the matron excused them but not before giving them a reminder to show up promptly for dinner duty.

As an afterthought, Ms. Sotto said, "And Andi, since you have no classes, come back after lunch and help with the dishes."

Chapter 15

After stacking the last dish into the cabinet, Andi had some free time before having to report back to the kitchen for the dinner shift. She decided to take advantage of the fact that Mrs. White was in Santa Barbara for the day.

The door to the administration office was closed. She tried the handle, but the place was obviously locked up. Too bad! Mrs. Huber had instructed her to send progress reports via e-mail whenever she had a chance to get her hands on a computer. Finding a way to access the Web in this place was not an easy task, she now realized. Taking a quick stab at the Whiz's office, she found the door wide open and glanced inside. He was not there, but she also knew that the head of the camp did not have a computer, at least not one set up on his desk. She looked behind her. There was nobody in sight, so she hurried to the end of the hallway. According to the matron, Doc was lunching elsewhere too, so Andi hoped he was not back yet. She tried his door - - it would not budge - - and remembered his telling her he kept it locked when absent.

When Andi was even with the Whiz's office once again, she decided to have a look. After all, he could keep a laptop hidden away. The coast was still clear, so she darted inside. She quickly opened his credenza but found only files and notes. Then she went over to the desk and, bingo, in the top drawer sat a laptop! Her excitement over finding the computer was short-lived as she grasped that the Whiz most certainly would have a password to open it up. Well, she would just have to wait until he was in the process of using it one day and maybe distract him. Fat chance, she muttered to herself.

She closed the desk drawer and was on her way out the door, when she heard voices coming from the front entrance. Shit, she thought, I can't be found in this part of the building without a good excuse, and sprinted into the staff's bathroom, locking the door behind her.

She resolved that she might as well "go." After flushing and washing her hands, she waited and listened. There was no sound coming from the corridor and she felt it was safe to leave. She slowly opened the door - - all was quiet - - and stepped into the hallway. Too late she saw the Whiz standing on the threshold of his office.

Like an oracle, he stated in his baritone, "The staff's bathroom is off limits to campers; I thought I made that clear!"

"Sorry, I forgot."

In a grave tone, he said, "Don't let it happen again."

Besides Andi, there were four more young people working to prepare the evening meal. It was soon evident that she was not about to get to know any of them. Everybody seemed tongue-tied under the strict supervision of the matron, and Andi wondered if silence would also have been kept in the kitchen had Mrs. White been presiding over their work.

Andi stared at the endless potato pile in front of her and wondered if these were the same potatoes she'd watched the group of inmates dig up. Peeling one after another, she thought, this is my third day at camp and I haven't done any successful detecting, let alone found Emily!

Chapter 16

The matron handed Andi her medication on Saturday morning and, watching her ingest it, said, "Doc Morrison is not a resident, but lives in Solvang and spends weekends with his family. So I'm handling your Antabuse treatment until Monday when he resumes your therapy sessions."

Andi replied, "He could've just given me the blasted tablets for today and tomorrow; I'm a big girl and can dissolve a pill in a glass of water."

Apparently unaware of the sarcasm in those words, Ms. Sotto said, "No, he couldn't do that. I am under order to only give you one tablet per day; we have to make sure that you don't overdose. I am also personally responsible to oversee that you actually take and swallow the medication."

Then she said, "The weekends are free for campers."

Andi thought, how free can they be? Aloud she asked, "Meaning?"

"No school, no farm work and chores - - with the exception of kitchen duty since we all have to eat - - and no therapy sessions with the Doc. You are free to pursue hobbies, stroll around the premises, read books, or engage in sports activities."

"Got it."

"And today is the first Saturday of the month, which means it's parent visiting day. Visiting hours are from after lunch until before dinner time, but that doesn't concern you as you're not eligible to have your parents visit for the first two months."

"It doesn't concern me, period."

"Oh, that's right; your parents are dead," she said, bluntly.

Is this woman made of stone? Andi wondered.

Chapter 17

Taking advantage of her freedom, Andi first strolled into the hobby room. A handful of kids were doing recreational activities. There was a camper who was twisting long, skinny balloons into balloon hats. Another was standing at an easel, painting the still-life scene of fruits and vegetables arranged on a small table next to him, and a third was stringing beads into a necklace. Over by the library section of the room, two girls were reading books, and a boy sat solving a Sudoku puzzle. There was a TV in the room, but it was turned off. The campers kept conversation at a minimum, most did not talk at all, and elevator music played softly in the background, almost putting Andi to sleep.

What's wrong with this picture? Andi mused. These are supposedly juvenile delinquents and they behave like little lambs. Her mind flashed back to how demure the kitchen duty crew had seemed the day before. All the kids she'd come across so far had been tame and conforming, with the exception of the two guys who'd gotten into a fight. Something's fishy in this place, she told herself. I just haven't figured it out yet.

Leaving the hobby room and stepping back into the hallway, Andi followed the sound of Hip Hop music and her stride became tuned to the rhythm with each additional step. Then she stood in the open doorframe of the music room taking in the performance that was unfolding before her eyes on the parquet floor.

Dewayne, the hood of his top pulled over his head and hiding part of his face, was too into his dance routine to notice Andi. He was doing the boogaloo with popping moves by quickly contracting and relaxing his muscles to cause a jerk. Then he changed his style and went into locking, using fast and sharp arm and hand movements followed by relaxed legs and hips. She watched as he changed from rapid motions into a 'locking' state, holding that position and then moving on to another step in the same speed as before. His movements were exaggerated and therefore comical, but always in perfect harmony with the beat.

When the music stopped and the dance came to a sudden halt, Andi clapped, which seemed to embarrass Dewayne. He said, "How long you been watching?"

"Not long enough," she replied. "That was awesome!"

"Do you Hip Hop?"

"Never tried it. Is it hard to learn?"

"Depends how fast you catch on! I'll teach you some day."

"I'd like that!" Andi replied.

As she walked to the kitchen for her lunch shift, she thought, Dewayne is acting natural enough and he's made my day. Maybe I've been imagining things earlier.

Chapter 18

In the afternoon, Andi gathered a few of her dirty pieces of clothing and went in search of the laundry room. Just as the matron had pointed out, the structure stood behind the main building. It looked similar to a public Laundromat; the only difference was that the machines lacked slots for inserting coins. The room had three rows of washers and jumbo-sized dryers lined up against the outer walls, a couple of tables for folding clothes, and a bench next to the entrance. Some of the machines were in use, but there were no people present when Andi entered. She dropped her load into an empty washer, grabbed liquid detergent from a shelf and poured some over the clothing, closed the lid and started the warm-wash cycle.

Then she sat down on the bench and mulled over the experiences of her last four days and soon focused on the unfinished sentence she had overheard on that first night, "...we have to kill the beast." Knowing the words had been uttered by either Mona or Tracy, she needed to find out whom they were talking about and why. It might have just been an innocent matter of speech and nothing more, although the whispered dialogue that preceded the statement had certainly been intense. It was also possible that she had misheard, since their voices had been barely audible.

"Welcome to wacko land!"

Andi practically jumped out of her seat. She had not heard or seen the young man coming who now stood in front of her.

"Sorry, I didn't mean to startle you. I'm Tyler, and I think the Whiz introduced you as Andi the other day."

She recovered fast and replied, "Yep, that's my name."

She looked him over as he went to dump his dirty laundry into a machine. He was lanky and trying to grow a goatee, which made his already narrow face look even longer.

When he joined her on the bench Andi asked, "Your folks didn't come today?"

"They live in Phoenix and seldom make it to parent visiting day."

"How long have you been here?"

"Forever! This is my second time at the camp. I was released, then had a relapse. I seem to be doing great while getting therapy, but then I can't handle the outside life." He paused and then added, "I think my parents have given up and decided to keep me locked up here and throw away the key."

There was sadness in his voice when he said that, so Andi tried to make a joke of it and remarked, "That'll cost them a bundle!"

"Yeah, this place isn't cheap. Most of us have rich parents, which proves that the privileged have the worst problem kids. There's two exceptions that I know of. Dewayne's mom uses the money she won in the lottery to pay for his fees, and Mike is an experiment the Social Services came up with."

"You mean the taxpayer is picking up his bill?"

"No, a private charity organization raised the money to send hard-to-handle kids who are under the government's care to places like Revamp Camp. I think the program is on a trial basis."

Andi was glad that she had finally stumbled on a camper that liked to talk, and said, "Tell me, Tyler, why did you call this place wacko land?"

He gave a nasty laugh and stated, "There are all sorts of bizarre people in our labor camp."

"You're talking about the campers?"

"Yeah, and staff too."

"Really?"

"Let me start at the top." He leaned toward her conspiratorially and said, "Everybody knows that the Whiz has supernatural powers like a sorcerer. Maybe you haven't been here long enough to experience it, but you'll see."

"Can't wait!" Andi put in.

He looked at her sharply to make sure that she wasn't mocking him. Satisfied, he continued, "The Whiz's wife hates our guts and wishes she could make us all go away. Then there's Elephant Ears, who - -"

"You mean Doc Morrison?"

"Who else? Anyhow, Elephant Ears locks himself up in his lab any chance he gets and mixes his poisonous concoctions like a mad scientist. He's trying to make headway in medical research and doesn't give a damn about how many rats he kills with his witch's brew. And I wouldn't be surprised if he uses humans as guinea pigs too."

Astonished, Andi asked, "You've seen his lab and he keeps rats in there?"

"Well, I didn't actually see them, but I heard noises coming out of the lab and they sounded like the squeaking of rats."

"Interesting!"

"Then there's Ratio D."

"Who or what is Ratio D?"

Grinning, Tyler replied, "Haven't figured that out yet myself, but I will!"

He went on, "I happen to know that the coach was involved in some shady dealings and was locked up for a while. As for the matron, I suspect that she's a closet smoker. I admit that I'm unaware of what darker secret lurks in her past, but I'm sure there is one. She's clearly sinister looking."

Andi thought that Tyler was a tad sinister looking himself, with his narrow features and sunken in eyes. And judging by his eerie assessment of the staff members, the kid also appeared to be one of his "wacko people."

A couple of campers came in and switched their laundry loads from washers to dryers without uttering a single word, and then left.

Tyler kept silent while the others were there but picked up his tale again as soon as they were out of earshot. He said, "I figure that our teacher, Roberta Ralston, is a fugitive from the law."

"How do you know?"

"She's terrified of meeting new people and goes into hiding whenever there are strangers at the camp. You won't see her today; she vanishes on parent visiting days."

"I haven't met Ms. Ralston and may never meet her since I'm not a student."

"Oh, you'll see her around; sometimes she even works in the fields."

He continued, "Gilmore, the math and science teacher, was sacked from a high school position because of a major scandal. I'm sure he hates it here but can't find a job anywhere else."

Andi's washer had stopped, and as she carried her few pieces of laundry to the dryer, Tyler commented, "You sure have a small load."

"And you're observant," she replied. "This is only my fourth day here, and I basically came to check out the laundry room."

She sat down next to him again, and he said, "As to campers, - -"

He didn't finish his sentence because Mike, the kid who had given Dewayne a bloody nose, appeared and said to Andi, "If he's telling you stories about witches and sorcerers, don't believe a word of it. All the drugs he used fried his brain." And with a sardonic smirk to Tyler, "I see you like older chicks."

Tyler did not respond, yet Andi could feel him stiffen next to her on the bench, obviously trying to control his anger. She came to his aid, making light of the other's remark, saying, "And he's got good taste too!"

Mike shrugged and went to get his laundry from the dryer. Watching him fold the clothes, she took in his physique. He was wiry, of medium height, and had a round face with light brown straight hair. Andi thought that he was above-average looking if you liked boyish baby faces with dimples; too bad that he seemed to have such a spiteful disposition.

As soon as Mike had left the laundry room, Tyler said, "There goes a vicious bully. I try to stay away from him as best I can, and you should too. He thinks he's superior because he's never been on drugs, except for his daily insulin injections, of course."

Andi asked, "Mike is diabetic?"

"Yeah, but that doesn't stop him from being the most hated guy in the entire camp. The only one who's not afraid of him is Dewayne. And Mike is after every girl camper that's not half bad looking; I suspect he's even raped a couple of them."

"You're jivin'!"

He went on, "Speaking of Dewayne, he is, or rather was, a gang member. Brandon, the guy you sit next to in the eatery, is a loner and kind of shy, but don't let that fool you. He attacked his mother with a butcher knife one day while spaced out and hallucinating. His old man came just in time to stop him before he wounded or killed her. Jacob, on your other side, is suicidal. I could tell you a lot more, but I think you get the picture about wacko land now."

"Sure do! How do you know all this stuff?"

He grinned again and replied, "Consider it my hobby. Doing projects in the hobby room isn't my bag, but finding out people's darkest secrets is."

"What do you know about Emily?"

"That kid is a mystery to me. So far I've had no luck with discovering what makes her tick. This much is clear, though: the girl is barely ticking!"

Andi's dryer had finished its cycle during Tyler's last revelation, and she was now holding her folded pieces of clothing in her arms, ready to leave.

She said, "Interestin' talking with you."

"Wait!"

Andi paused with one foot already out the door and turned her head back toward him.

"What's *your* secret?"

"Wouldn't you like to know!" she answered, and kept going.

When she was placing the clean laundry inside her locker in the girls' scrub room, her head was spinning with Tyler's outrageous stories. That boy sure has a vivid and wild imagination, she mused. He must be reading or watching too much science fiction fantasies. Still, she supposed that some of what he told her was true. All she had to do was weed out facts from fabrications. And what did he mean with his remark that Emily "was barely ticking"? Andi asked herself.

Chapter 19

At their Merida residence, R. A. Huber stepped out of a room which had served different purposes at various times. It had been labeled play-and-games room when their kids were growing up, later it was called the sewing room, and for the last decade it became the computer room. She closed the door behind her and joined her husband in the den on Saturday evening.

Peter gazed up from his laptop and said, "You look frustrated; I take it that there is no news from Andi."

"No, I just checked my e-mail inbox again and am getting worried."

"She probably just hasn't found a way to access the Internet yet or has nothing earthshaking to report, so don't get upset, Regula."

"Have you heard from Roger Hawk in the last few days, and did he talk with his daughter in the meantime?"

Peter replied, "Yes to question number one and no to number two."

"See!" she exclaimed. "Both Emily and Andi could have been abducted, and we'd never know about it."

"It's totally far-fetched to suspect anything of that sort at this point. Be reasonable. Andi went there on Wednesday and today is only Saturday."

"Okay," his spouse stated, "I'll give it a week, and if I haven't any news by this coming Wednesday, I need to find a way to check out Revamp Camp for myself."

Then she came closer and looked at his laptop over his shoulder. Peter always kept his stories secret from her before they were published, and she never had any idea of what they were about until the books came off the press.

Teasing him, she said, "Let me know if you want any feedback about your new manuscript."

"Good try! That reminds me, how about a visit to Europe, say, end of September or beginning of October?"

"Where in Europe?"

"I have Madrid and Barcelona in mind, but we can take a side trip to Switzerland, if you like."

Regula thought that it was interesting the way they now referred to their native country as simply Switzerland. Years ago, Peter would have said, "We can take a side trip home." She mused, we've made our home in the United States for so long that we consider ourselves full-fledged Americans.

She said, "Sounds great, but don't make reservations yet."

"Surely by fall your juvenile delinquent case will be over and done with."

She didn't answer, and he gazed into her eyes and then said, "You're still anxious. I have a good remedy to calm your nerves. Let's go to bed and I'll show you what I mean."

As they walked down the hallway, Regula remarked, "Madrid and Barcelona, hmm." And knowing good and well that he would keep her in the dark about his current manuscript, she couldn't resist and said, "Are you doing research about bullfighting, flamenco dancing, or do you want to give the reader a first-hand account of strolling down La Rambla?"

"You never give up, do you?" Peter said with a chuckle as they reached the bedroom.

Chapter 20

A Catholic, Andi had been brought up to regard the essence and most important part of Sunday Mass as the Mass itself; in other words, what went on at the altar. In practice, what really drew her to attend was the singing. She loved to sing to her heart's content; whether in Latin, French or English made no difference. The only other place she was able to let her vocal chords run wild was in the shower. At Revamp Camp, she felt reluctant to sing in the shower with other girls bathing and using the facilities all around her. With that in mind, Andi was looking forward to the service in the assembly hall on Sunday morning.

Before ambling over to the spiritual gathering, she checked the chore-schedule in the hallway and saw her name listed on the board. She was assigned to work in the school building and ordered to report to Ms. Sotto in the study hall on Monday. She smiled to herself, thinking, I don't have latrine duty after all.

Three dozen folding chairs were set up in neat rows in the assembly hall. About half the seats were already taken when Andi entered, and she found an empty one on the third row from the pulpit. She asked the kid seated next to her if he was familiar with the service and whether she could look forward to lots of singing. He explained that the presiding rectors changed each Sunday so the service was never the same, and there was no singing as far as he knew. Before long, the Whiz appeared with another man in tow.

He walked up to the podium and said, "Please welcome our speaker for today, Brother Bob," handed the microphone over, and stepped down.

Brother Bob took charge and spoke nonstop for nearly an hour. He was a nondescript sort of guy, soft-spoken and amiable, but had little of substance to say. He must have been instructed to leave any mention of deity or prophets out of his sermon and was careful not to use words such as God, Jesus, Christ, Messiah, Lord, Allah, Mohamed, Buddha, and so forth. It was meant to be an inspirational talk about giving a helping hand to your fellow man and peace on earth, but with his monotonous tone of voice, the man seemed unable to motivate and inspire his audience.

Andi had not expected to hear Bible readings or any kind of traditional ceremony; after all, this was a generic service. Still, she felt let down as she listened to Brother Bob. Then she studied the faces of the kids around her and was shocked. They sat in their seats like zombies, expressionless and devoid of emotion.

Suddenly, Andi did not miss the singing any longer; she had lost all desire for merriment.

Chapter 21

On that Sunday afternoon, Roberta Ralston sat at the desk in her bedroom suite preparing students' lessons for the coming week. She could have chosen to do this in her classroom or the study hall of the adjacent school building, but felt more comfortable staying in the privacy of her own room. The twenty-eight-year-old teacher was of average height and weight, wore her light-brown hair in a bun, and hid her hazel eyes behind gold-rimmed glasses. Her main objective in the last few years had been to blend into the woodwork and avoid drawing attention to herself.

She tried to concentrate on the subject matter of English, history and geography, but her mind kept wandering. She had been at the facility three years already, teaching all high school level curriculum, except math and science. With something close to panic, she realized that her days seemed wasted in this place. The pay was good and Mr. and Mrs. White treated her well, even though Mr. White - - she could never bring herself to calling him the Whiz - - was overbearing at times. The students were a different matter. Most of them lacked true interest in learning and just went through the motions of attending class. As a dedicated educator, this was painful for her to witness.

She sighed and thought, I'm rotting away at this camp trying to hide from the outside world. It had seemed a haven to her three years ago and she'd felt safe here, but now she started to feel like a prisoner within the compound's walls. Yet whenever she ventured outside, she needed to be on constant guard like a watch-dog, which was tiresome. Yesterday, she came back from her shopping trip to Solvang emotionally exhausted.

On the other hand, I can't stay concealed here indefinitely, she reasoned. I'm still young and should allow myself some fun now and then. And a sad little simper escaped her mouth as she thought, that isn't likely to happen in this place of tightly controlled isolation. I had no choice but to cut all strings to the past and start a new life, but am I really *living* at Revamp Camp?

With a final sigh, she forced her mind back to preparing the lessons for her students.

Chapter 22

Coach Kyle Norton dismissed the team and walked away from baseball practice making a face like he'd just bitten into a lemon. He thought, these kids are not ready to take on the visiting team in two weeks by a long shot. And the Whiz couldn't have chosen a worse time to suspend my two star players. Of course, there have to be strict rules in the camp, but it's only natural for boys to get into fights. If it was up to him, he would make an exception and let Mike and Dewayne play. Without them, we haven't the slightest chance against the opposition, he thought. Disgusted, he knew that bringing it up with the Whiz would be useless; they had gone that route before. His boss felt that being consistent in punishment was more important than winning a game.

Not for the first time, Kyle got furious with himself and the world at large when he dwelled on what could have been. By now his proper place should have been coaching the major leagues, not wasting his time and talent on some brats who didn't give a damn about baseball. Last month he had turned forty, and what did he have to show for it? Was he destined to spend the rest of his life out of sight at Revamp Camp?

He had only himself to blame. Things would have turned out differently had he resisted taking that bribe. Yet he had paid his dues in serving a prison term and in all fairness was owed a decent life after his release. In the real world, you could not pick up where you had left off, ever again. He saw no chance of furthering his career and was stuck here. The pay was good, no complaints there, but he hated everything about this place. The more he thought about his dilemma, the more desperate he got.

When he'd walked away from the baseball field in a fit of anger, he hadn't paid attention of where he was going. Now he was surprised to find himself trudging on the dirt road leading around the camp fields. He glanced at the neat columns of vegetables growing all around him and his rage welled up once more. I'm a coach and not a farmer, for Pete's sake! Yes, when he hired me, the Whiz made me sign a contract in which I promised to help with the crops when needed. At the time, I had no idea what that entailed, but I sure learned in a hurry. He kicked some pebbles out of his way and thought, I don't even have my own room but sleep in a dorm supervising a bunch of toughs.

Next his thoughts turned to his non-existent love-life. The only eligible adult females in this place are Heather Sotto and Roberta Ralston, he grumbled. The idea of thinking about the matron in a romantic way gave him the willies; he wasn't that desperate. Now the little teacher was a different matter. He felt positive that beneath that prim and proper surface was a sensual woman. Too bad that she's unapproachable.

Then he stopped his train of thought and listened. Sounds like a motorcycle! I must be going nuts; there are no motorbikes at the camp.

Chapter 23

Andi was thrilled to be straddled on her Harley again. Assuming that the Whiz had long forgotten or changed his mind about letting her ride, she was speechless when he came looking for her suggesting she take her bike for a spin. He said it would be on a trial basis and spelled the rules out for her, and she happily promised not to break any of them.

So he had ordered Mrs. White to push the appropriate button to release the main gate, and Andi had enjoyed a brief moment of freedom as she walked through it to fetch her bike. Once on the dirt lot, she gave the Harley's handlebar an affectionate slap, the way one would greet an old friend. Then she swung one long leg over the saddle, kicked the kickstand up, hit the starter button and put it into gear. As soon as she had cleared the entrance gate, it snapped shut behind her once more with that ominous thud.

Now she rode on the trail encircling the entire property, but this time going around it from the opposite direction she had walked with the Whiz. She started at the main gate and went along the front of the building, then took the route to the left. The bike performed well on the narrow dirt road, but the terrain required her full concentration as she couldn't afford to slip on loose gravel. At times, the track took her close by the lower fence of the compound and then led inward again.

Soon she came upon rows and rows of citrus trees and stopped the bike for a moment to take it all in. Then she examined the nearest tree. Yep, those are lemons, and I bet the trees farther away are laden with oranges, she told herself. Continuing her ride, she came to realize how huge the place was. The Whiz mentioned 150 acres, but since she was neither a rancher nor a real estate agent, the number had meant little to her.

Coming out of the semi-circle at the end of the property, she was again astonished to find such a large vineyard spreading along the hillside of the estate. Before she reached the vegetable patch, a lone man walked toward her from the opposite direction. Andi did not want to kick dust in his face and stalled the bike, waiting for him to pass. He was six feet tall and husky, and there was an athletic spring to his gait. A mop of curly light-brown hair escaped from beneath his baseball cap. As he got closer, Andi recognized him as the coach.

When even with her, he said, "How the heck did you smuggle a motorcycle into the camp?"

She grinned and replied, "Got permission from the Whiz!"

"Unbelievable! And how did you manage that?"

"Simple. I told him that ridin' the Harley is my hobby."

He laughed out loud and then said, "The Whiz is big on hobbies! So he lets you ride it as often as you want?"

"No sir, only in my free time," and with a mischievous glint in her eyes she added, "Reckon not being a student I'll have plenty of that."

Again he chuckled, and it felt good after his previous gloomy mood He said, "You're Andi, right?"

"Sure am. And you're the coach, but I don't know your name."

"It's Kyle Norton, but you may call me Coach."

Then Andi remarked, "I gather that we're self-sufficient with produce, and if we were all vegetarians, there'd be no dependency on the outside world at all."

"That'll never happen."

"What won't?"

"That everyone becomes vegetarian. I, for one, love my meat."

"So where's the Whiz hidin' the cattle, pigs and chickens?"

"Never gave it a thought," he joked back.

Andi said, "Well, I'd best be on my way; it's getting too warm to idle in my leather jacket and gloves. You go first, Coach, so you don't swallow my dust."

After having walked a few paces, he turned his head and called out to her, "Wait! Are you any good at baseball?"

"Afraid not; shooting baskets is more my speed."

"That figures," he said under his breath.

Chapter 24

During Monday morning's therapy session with Doc Morrison, Andi was telling a duck-hunting story that she had experienced with Daddy, when four horn blasts nearly jolted her off the patient chair.

Doc said, "We need to cut your session short today. You have five minutes to get to the assembly hall."

"What's happening there?"

"The Whiz gives a camper pep talk every Monday, sort of energizing everyone for the coming week."

Andi got up to leave and asked, "Do I come back to your office afterwards?"

"No," he replied, "I'll be working in the lab, so we'll continue the session tomorrow."

When Andi reached the opposite wing of the building, she joined the stream of campers in the hallway who flocked to the assembly hall. Once inside, she observed that the folding chairs were neatly stacked against the wall again, and it became clear that this was a "standing" gathering. Within minutes, the room filled with chatting teens and they all stopped talking when the Whiz appeared. There was suddenly total silence; the only sound that could be heard was the Whiz's footsteps when he walked to the podium.

He looked impressive as always. His ponytail gleamed with freshly washed hair and there was an electrifying force coming from the steel-gray eyes as he addressed his audience.

"Good morning, campers!"

"Good morning, Whiz!" the kids shouted back in a chorus.

Then he started his spiel, "Our goal is for each and every one of you to eventually leave Revamp Camp as responsible and productive young adults. You can accomplish this by abiding by the rules, getting therapy and various treatments, and most importantly, by doing lots of hard work." He paused and stared at his campers.

They called out simultaneously, "Yes, Whiz!"

"This week, let's focus on - -"

The pep talk continued in that manner, and whenever the Whiz wanted to emphasize a point, he either paused in his monologue for a second, or said something like, "Is that clear?" and, "Are you cool with that?" Then the kids would shout, "Yes, Whiz!" in response.

Andi stopped listening and looked around. The young people seemed to hang on the Whiz's every word. It was true that he had a forceful personality and tremendous charisma, but there was more to it than that. These kids appeared mesmerized. Could he possibly be hypnotizing them? Judging by the stars in their eyes, it was entirely possible. She glanced over to where Mona and Tracy stood; both girls appeared to be in a trance.

Some inmates seemed unaffected, but they were clearly in the minority. Dwayne was close by, and as she glanced at his face, Andi was certain that the Whiz's lecture left him cold. Also, when she made eye contact with Mike, he actually winked at her.

When Andi stepped out of the assembly hall a good half hour later, she felt a tad light-headed. It was not so much *what* the Whiz had said in his speech but rather *how* he had said it. There was no denying that the man had the gift of enticing people to take his every word as gospel truth and that by sheer power of personality he was able to alter their frame of mind. But when Andi tried to recapture the essence of his lecture, she could not remember a single sentence.

Chapter 25

The study hall was a gigantic room inside the school building furnished with student desks and chairs arranged in eight rows of five. Name tags were affixed to each study space. At the head of the room, there was a large supervisor desk erected on a platform. It was at that desk that Heather Sotto sat engrossed in her story about Amazon women warriors.

When coming to the end of a chapter, she looked up from her book and stared unseeing at the empty student desks in front of her, thinking, I wish that I was an Amazon. What great, courageous women they were! Then she forced herself back into reality and mused, I really have no cause to complain. Life at Revamp Camp suits me. I enjoy the power of being in charge of the campers and need not take orders from anyone, except from the Whiz. I don't even mind the manual labor in the fields, and I have plenty of free time. There's no way I could find such a well paying job elsewhere without a college education.

Her reflections were interrupted as Andi bounced into the study hall, saying, "Ms. Sotto! I'm supposed to report to you for duty."

The matron shut her book closed with a bang and said, "Then let's get with it!"

She stood up, came down from her platform, and when she was eye to eye with Andi continued, "You are assigned to keep house in the school building. Today, you'll tackle the study hall here. Tomorrow, you'll clean Ms. Ralston's classroom; on Wednesday, Mr. Gilmore's; Thursday, the school building's bathrooms; and on Friday, the hallways. Got it?"

"Sure thing! And then the next week I'll start all over again?"

"No, smarty pants, by then you'll be assigned to other duties; they'll be most likely farm chores."

Then Ms. Sotto looked up at the large clock on the wall and stated, "It is nearly 10:30. At 3:30 in the afternoon the study hall has to be accessible to the students for doing homework. I want you to be done and out of here by three o'clock. You can take an hour for lunch, so that leaves you with three and a half hours, which is adequate time to do the job. You'll find dust cloths, polish, brooms, mops, and whatever else you'll need in the hall closet next to the girls' bathroom."

So under the matron's supervision, Andi washed finger prints and smudges off the walls, and then dusted and polished the 30 or so desks and chairs. After lunch, she sat the chairs on top of each desk to make the floor ready for cleaning. Then she swept, mopped, and finally polished it. At five minutes to three her chores were done.

Ms. Sotto looked up from her book and said, "You're free to leave." And as Andi walked toward the door, she asked, "What are you going to do with the rest of the afternoon?"

"Reckon I'll be ridin' some," Andi replied with a grin.

Chapter 26

After dinner that evening, Andi ambled into the hobby room and found Mona engrossed in a project. She had the room to herself and was working on the finishing touches of a miniature dollhouse. Andi was not sure if she was welcome and watched from a distance. The dollhouse was actually a big boot, the idea taken from the Mother Goose nursery rhyme, "There was an old woman who lived in a shoe."

Mona suddenly straightened, and glancing up from painting a small piece of elongated balsa wood, said, "Oh, it's you!"

"Mind if I have a look?"

"No, come closer. The dollhouse itself is done; I'm constructing stuff I'm going to add to the front yard."

Andi examined the "shoe-dollhouse" and was enchanted with its exquisite beauty and detail. Looking through the windows of the boot enabled her to explore the miniature living room and kitchen downstairs, and the bedroom and bath on the upper story. A couple of children-dolls were placed in the kitchen, baking cookies in a stainless steel oven. The living room was decked out with a brocade sofa, wooden coffee table, and an entire wall with a built-in bookcase, as well as a grandfather clock. The "old woman" doll sat in a rocker with a throw folded over her lap, holding a storybook that she was obviously reading to the many children scattered all around her.

Upstairs, the bedroom was outfitted with a wardrobe, a mirror/dresser, and night stand, and the four-poster bed was full of sleeping kids. The adjacent bathroom sported a footed tub, pedestal sink and a toilet, all done in ceramic with a hand-painted, embossed rosebud pattern and gold faucets. The rugs, as well as towels hanging on a rack, were pink. Andi got a special kick out of the three children mounting the staircase between the two stories, giving the impression that they were on their way to bed.

A little house was attached to the top of the boot, which gave it an attic effect. Peeking inside through the attic window, she glimpsed a piano and a harp with two miniature dolls sitting at the instruments giving a concert.

Andi exclaimed, "Wow! I'm impressed. What's it made of?"

Mona replied, "Most people use Styrofoam or wood to make dollhouses that need to be carved out with an x-acto knife. Mine is made with papier-mâché and I can use scissors."

"I take it the Whiz doesn't like sharp knives 'round here."

"You got that right."

"How did you go about building your shoe-house?"

Mona had finished painting the little piece of wood and set the brush aside. She was happy to be showing off her creation but did not want to look eager with enthusiasm.

She said in her usual gruff manner, "I'll explain it to you if you're really interested."

"Sure am!"

"I started off with the boot, which I ordered from a crafts catalogue. Like I already said, the boot is made from papier-mâché. All I had to do is paint it brown. Constructing the outside was easy; I used a piece of leather for the tongue and workman's boot laces. As for building the interior, I cut the window openings first before making the layout for the ground floor with a divider between the living room and kitchen. Then I made the separation between stories by gluing in a heavy piece of cardboard, which is the ceiling for the lower and floor for the upper level.

"All the walls are made from heavy cardboard, and I used lightweight Plexiglas for the windows, which I took from tops of Christmas card boxes. The carpets are cut-out fabric pieces, and the wallpaper is simply gift-wrapping paper. Some of the furniture, fixtures and accessories I made, and others I bought from dollhouse catalogues. Several of their items had to be assembled and painted. I made the bookshelf and all the books in it myself, by the way."

"Did you make the dolls?"

"No, I bought them, but I made their outfits."

Mona continued, "I built the small house that sits on top of the boot separately and then glued it on. It's made of heavy cardboard with construction paper siding and shingles."

Pointing to the windows on the house, she said, "I used balsa wood for creating the mullions."

"Mullions are the little cross bars that divide window lights, right?"

She nodded and went on, "In case you're wondering what the window outlines are made from, I cut them out of doily and then painted them brown. I made a template first for each row of construction paper shingles."

Andi remarked, "I just now notice that there's a balcony at one side of the house. How did you make the railing for it?"

"I used lace and then painted it to make it stiff."

"I've seen miniature dollhouses before, but this one seems especially small. What is the scale?"

"The usual dollhouse is an inch to the foot, but I made mine in quarter inch to the foot scale. Everything matches that scale. The dolls are about an inch tall or four feet in the real world."

"So what's the thing you just painted?"

"That's part of the teeter-totter. I'm going to add a playground in the front yard of the shoe, with a slide, swing, teeter-totter and sandbox."

Andi said, "Thanks for sharing your craft with me!" Then she studied the feisty girl for a moment and added, "You're an amazing artist, but I'm mostly blown away by your patience working with these tiny objects."

Mona answered with typical attitude, "What you mean is, how come a tough broad like me is interested in making dollhouses?"

"Something like that."

There was a long silence and then Mona finally said, "Okay, consider yourself privileged; I don't tell my story to many people. The fact is that I've always craved a big family with lots of siblings. The old lady living in the shoe with all her kids is my fantasy."

She paused again, and Andi encouraged her by saying, "And you are an only child?"

She nodded and continued, "You'd think that an only kid would be pampered and given lots of attention, but I was mostly ignored. Both my parents have big careers and those always come first. After they divorced, I seldom saw my father, and mom was busier than ever. During my elementary school years I had a nanny who was nice but boring. Once in junior high and high school, I mostly fended for myself. After-school sports kept me content for a while, but eventually I hung with the wrong crowd and started using drugs. Then it got out of hand and became a full-blown addiction."

"I hear ya! With me it was alcohol," Andi put in, living her role.

"Mom makes plenty of money, but never gave me a big allowance. I had to keep records and answer to her for every dollar I spent. At first my druggie friends treated me, but that didn't last long, and I had to come up with my own cash. I did odd jobs for people in my neighborhood for a while, like weeding gardens and doggy-sitting, but that was just peanuts. As my cocaine habit got worse, I needed a steady income. I ended up working the streets to pay for my drugs."

"You became a hooker?"

"Yeah, for a few months. Then my mom got wise to it and unloaded me here. End of story."

"And what a story it is! Are you happy here?"

She grinned and said, "I found a great hobby!"

"Besides that?"

Mona reverted to her brazen self and retorted, "No, I'm not happy here. But then I've never been happy, so what's the difference?"

Andi's expression became grave when she said, "I'd like to talk to you about what I overheard on my first night here."

Mona shot her an anxious glance and asked, "What do you mean?"

"I heard you whisper about killing someone."

"Oh, that was just make-believe girl talk. We weren't serious."

"Your exact words were, 'We have to kill the beast.' Who is the beast?"

The small brunette's eyes darted to the open door as she replied, "Don't make a big deal out of this. We were just pretending; it means nothing."

Andi shrugged and said, "I'll ask Tracy, then. She was the other person whispering in your bunk, right?"

"You leave Tracy alone, you hear! She's already scared enough."

"What's she afraid of?"

"Getting caught, of course. I'm sure you read the dorm rules: *No visiting in each other's bunks.*"

At that moment the Whiz stuck his head in the door and said, "Have you seen Ms. Sotto?"

Mona replied, "No, Whiz. I think she's on duty in the study hall."

"Thanks," he said, and was gone.

Without another word, Mona gathered together her dollhouse, teeter-totter part, paint, brush and balsa wood, and stowed everything in her allotted cabinet space.

On leaving the hobby room she stated, "Might as well hang in the study hall too and get some homework done."

Chapter 27

Left alone in the hobby room, Andi was about to turn the TV on but dismissed the idea and went out into the hallway, where she heard the sound of a piano being played. The door to the music chamber was ajar and she gently pushed it open, then stood and listened, fascinated. Jacob was playing a most haunting tune, unlike any she had ever listened to before. Andi was strangely moved by his music.

When his long fingers came to a halt and the last note still hung in the air, she stepped closer and said, "That was a touching melody. What's it called?"

Jacob replied, "I haven't named it yet; so far the lyrics are vaguely floating around in my head."

"You composed that song yourself?" she asked in amazement.

He nodded.

"You're a genius!"

"I hate that word," he said with sudden force. And ignoring her, he started playing a classical piece that Andi had heard before, although she couldn't remember the name or composer. He ended with a rapid succession of scales and then abruptly stopped.

He said, "Sorry for snapping at you, but I became a child prodigy at eight and my life has turned to shit ever since."

She looked into his sad eyes and said, "I didn't mean to stir things up for you."

"I'm used to it; in therapy Doc Morrison stirs things up all the time."

"Does it help you any?"

"Sometimes."

Andi figured that he would clam up if she probed and said, "I'll understand if you don't want to talk about it."

He seemed to mull things over and then said, "I don't mind telling you," and began with the tragic story of his young life.

"I gave my first solo concert when I was ten and from then on, life in the limelight never ended. I was either on tour or preparing for the next performance. Since I was on the move a lot and a good part of my day was taken up with practicing, my parents took me out of public school and hired private tutors. There wasn't ever time for fun and games; I was either alone or doted on by adults. I missed out on kid stuff."

"I hear ya!"

"Don't get me wrong; I loved my music and still do, but I never liked to perform. My parents, music teacher, and agent all pushed me to maximum achievements. To keep the momentum up despite a lack of sleep on a regular basis, I took amphetamines. Eventually this led to depression. I didn't want to disappoint my parents, who were so proud of me, so I kept on plugging away, concert after concert. By the time I was sixteen, my addiction to uppers and downers was out of control and I became suicidal. I ended up in the hospital while on tour in Europe, but I don't want to get into all that."

Andi asked, "Are you getting better here at Revamp Camp?"

"Yes and no."

"Meaning?"

"I'm under no pressure to perform, which is a great relief, and I'm almost drug free, but I can't shake the feeling that I'm being programmed."

"Programmed how?"

"I can't explain it." Then he looked down at the keys in front of him and asked, "Do you play?"

"The fiddle's all I know."

"Maybe you and I can try a duet one day."

"I didn't bring my fiddle."

"Oh, I'm sure the Whiz keeps a violin in one of the closets in this room."

Andi said, "Speaking of the Whiz, do you like him?"

Jacob's face took on a solemn expression when he replied, "Everybody likes the Whiz."

Settled in her upper bunk that night, Andi pondered the two sad stories she had been told, and a moment before falling asleep she murmured, Daddy, if you can hear me, thank you for my happy childhood!

Chapter 28

On Tuesday morning, R. A. Huber drove to her Pasadena office with the intention of doing some long overdue paperwork and paying bills. Now, she was absentmindedly fingering a black Bishop of the Staunton Rosewood chessmen set up on the chessboard at one end of her desk. Instead of writing checks, her mind dwelled on Andi, imagining all sorts of dangers her young assistant could possibly find herself in at Revamp Camp. The ringing of the phone interrupted her dark thoughts.

"Private investigating, R. A. Huber. How may I help you?"

"It's me."

"Oh Peter! What's up?"

"I just heard from Roger Hawk. He finally had a phone conversation with Emily."

"That is great news!"

"Not altogether."

"Why not? What did Emily say?"

"That's just it; she didn't talk."

"You're not making any sense, Peter. How could they have a phone conversation and she not talk?"

"According to Roger, his daughter sounded muddled. He barely got "yes" and "no" answers out of her. He is worried and thinks there is something drastically wrong with her."

"That settles it!" his wife burst out. "I'm going to Revamp Camp."

After they hung up, Huber mulled over possible ways to gain access to the place. Posing as a social worker had first come to mind, but she soon rejected the idea, since she was certain that credentials would be checked. She was too old to pass as the parent of a prospective camper wishing to check the site out. Then she had an idea that seemed feasible; I may get away with posing as a journalist interested in doing a story about the facility.

She went over to the file cabinet and got out the Revamp Camp folder. Going over its meager content, she murmured to herself, "Let's see if Mr. White is up for some free publicity for his place," and reached for the phone.

Chapter 29

Since Andi's job was to clean Ms. Ralston's classroom when school was out in the late afternoon, she moved up the bike ride to her free time after lunch. Despite the fact that Solvang was experiencing days of above average temperatures, Andi was wearing her leather jacket, gloves, cowboy boots, goggles and helmet for protection. Even though she could not crank up the speed on the dirt roads and pathways inside the camp, a false move on the gravel could easily make her spin out and fall. The less skin exposed, the better for her.

On that Tuesday's ride, she was exploring the areas between the lower and upper stretch of the main road leading around the compound. She chose a narrow connecting pathway traversing the width of the property and came upon an orchard. From a distance, she spotted a figure sitting under one of the apple trees. Upon riding closer, she recognized the person as a girl she had seen in the dormitory.

Andi stopped and waved to her, but the girl did not wave back. There was no reaction at all; she just sat there motionless, like a statue. Andi thought this was strange since the camper had to have heard the sound of her

Harley approaching, unless she was deaf. Suddenly, she had a hunch of who this might be. So she killed the engine, parked the bike on the trail, and then walked over to the girl. She sat bolt upright on the bare ground with her shoulder-length ash-blond hair disheveled, and the light-blue eyes unfocused and dull.

Andi said, "I see you found a shady spot!"

There was no response.

"What's your name?"

Again, there was only silence.

Could the girl really be deaf, Andi wondered. While taking off her helmet and goggles, she stepped near her and bent down, then, putting her face two inches away from the other's, asked, "Are you Emily?"

The closeness seemed to shock the girl out of her trance. She made eye contact with Andi and replied, "Yes."

"Nice to meet ya. I'm Andi."

"Hi."

"Betcha you're dyin' to know what I'm doing at the camp."

Emily just stared.

"Have you been here long?"

"I don't know."

"I mean under this tree."

She shrugged as if to say she had no idea.

"Are you feeling all right?"

She didn't answer and Andi felt that the girl was retreating into her own world again.

"I think you should see Doc Morrison."

"I did."

"You had a treatment today?"

Emily did not answer but said, "I want to be alone now."

"Well, nice chatting with you!"

Andi rode off thinking; I finally met Emily and there is plenty wrong with her. I wish I knew what and why.

A little farther up, Andi ran into Mike. He was striding in the same direction on the trail ahead of her, then turned around when he heard her coming. She slowed down to a walking tempo in order not to kick up dust and raised her gloved hand in greeting as she was about to pass him. All of a sudden, he jumped in front of her, blocking her way. She screeched to a halt, nearly losing her balance.

"That was stupid; I could've hurt you!"

He said sarcastically, "Do you see me shaking with fear?" Then he said, "Give me a ride to the school building; I'm late for math class."

"Can't do that. One of the Whiz's rules when he gave me permission to ride was, *absolutely no passengers.*"

"Come now, you're not afraid of the Whiz. I watched you during his pep talk and you were too busy studying other campers to get caught up in the Whiz's spell."

"I noticed you were not affected either."

"It takes more than a little hoodoo to impress me," Mike shot back.

Then he leaned over the bike's handlebars toward her and hissed, "I heard that chicks from New Orleans are easy, especially redheads!"

An angry flicker loomed in Andi's green eyes as she ordered, "Get out of my way!" and at the same time accelerated.

Mike cursed and jumped aside in the nick of time and then swallowed a mouthful of dust as Andi sped away, shouting, "Nobody likes a bully!"

Mike spat out the bad taste in his mouth and, shaking his fist, yelled after her, "I'll get you for this, you bitch!"

Chapter 30

Two hours later, Andi had time for a quick shower before having to report for duty in Ms. Ralston's classroom. It felt good to get rid of the dust mixed with sweat, she thought, as the water hit her and she was working up shower-gel lather.

Down the hallway, Mike was cleaning a toilet in the boys' scrub room and was not a happy camper. Not only had the Whiz expelled him from the baseball team, but also ordered extra chores. Latrine duty was the most demeaning of them all. True, Dewayne was scrubbing toilets downstairs in the staff bathroom, but that's no consolation, Mike thought.

Then he listened; did he hear the shower being used in the girls' scrub room? I must be imagining it. Who would take a shower in the middle of the day? Moments later, he was sure. There was no doubt that the sound he heard was of running water coming from a showerhead. He interrupted his work and walked along the corridor to investigate. Just as he pushed the door to the girls' scrub room open, the water was turned off in one of the shower stalls. He stood in the doorway, waiting.

So it's the red-haired bitch! he thought, as Andi stepped out of the stall reaching for her towel and walked to locker number eight. She rubbed her hair in the towel first, then dried her body and put on bra and panties. Then she turned around and noticed him.

"Holy Krewe! What are *you* doin' here?"

He entered, closing the door behind him, and licking his lips advanced toward her, saying, "I knew I'd get to you sooner or later," and with an ugly grin he added, "I thank my lucky stars it's sooner!"

From the moment Andi had first caught sight of him, she knew what he was up to. He was athletic and strong, so she needed to be quick and precise if she wanted to get away unharmed. She had been biding time with her silly question and while he was giving his snide answer, planning her strategy of how best to render him powerless.

Mike approached and grabbed her by the arm. He obviously expected her to try to pull away, but instead, Andi launched into him, using her entire body. The force of her movement nearly made him lose his balance, but he recovered fast and tightened the grip on her arm. Andi smashed her free elbow into his ribs, followed by a good knee to his groin. With an ear-piercing cry of pain, he let go of her arm and fell to the ground.

Andi calmly finished dressing, blew-dry her hair, and when she was ready to leave, Mike was still lying in the same spot, writhing.

She stepped over him and remarked, "Hope you learned a lesson, you jerk!"

Chapter 31

James and Doreen White were enjoying a salmon dinner at a restaurant by the ocean in Morro Bay. To Doreen's delight, they had been given a window table. Looking out to sea, she noticed that the famous rounded rock sticking out of the water, which had been there earlier when they strolled along the marina, had vanished. It was apparently engulfed by fog. Doreen was aware that James had planned their outing to pacify her, but she decided to take what she could get and enjoyed the moment.

She watched the sea lions resting on a float a few yards away. There were five of them, and close enough that she could study their faces. To her surprise, they did not all look alike; each wore a different expression.

She reached across the table and, placing her hand on top of James', said, "Thanks for bringing me here today; I've had a wonderful time!"

"It's not over yet," he replied with a twinkle in his eye.

While Doreen savored the last bite of her spumoni dessert, he said, "That woman who called this morning is a newspaper reporter with Spy Gazette."

"Never heard of it!"

"Evidently it's a brand-new paper. Anyhow, I decided to let her do an article about Revamp Camp."

"Really?"

"She said that her paper is doing an on-going segment about troubled youth, and that she is doing interviews at several different rehabilitation facilities for juveniles."

"Interesting."

He continued, more to himself, it seemed, "We might benefit from the publicity. I'll lay down the ground rules, of course, when she gets to the camp tomorrow."

"She's coming tomorrow?"

"Yes. Do you have a problem with that?"

"Not me!" she replied, mocking him. "Anything to kill the monotony."

James gave her a piercing stare with his steel-gray eyes and said, "So you're still dwelling on your baby kick. How about if I get you a puppy instead?"

Doreen was furious and rendered speechless for a second, but then she broke out in a torrent of accusations, "Don't patronize me! I am not one of your juveniles where you can pull strings as if they were marionettes. Don't you dare make fun of me and suggest a dog as a replacement for a child! I'll fight you to the end on this!"

She had become louder and louder, and people at surrounding tables were gawking. Her husband paid the bill, adding a generous tip to make up for her outburst, and they left in haste.

Neither spoke on the hour-and-a-half drive home. Doreen thought, we had such a great outing and then he had to ruin it all, while the man at the wheel thought, she is getting more and more ridiculous.

Chapter 32

When Andi walked into Doc Morrison's office on Wednesday morning, the armoire-bar was wide open with all the bottles of booze in full display. Neither of them commented on that fact. The doctor gave Andi her Antabuse drink as she sat down to her psychiatric therapy session, which habitually lasted about half an hour. They had established a routine where she would talk about anything that entered her head. So far, she had been careful to stay within her role as a troubled young woman with an alcohol problem.

She now asked, "Do you keep rats in your lab?"

"Rats! Whatever gives you that idea?"

"Tyler thinks you do."

He smiled and replied, "You can't take Tyler seriously; he's got a wild imagination."

At that moment Doc's i-phone rang, and after checking its message, he got to his feet and said, "I'll be right back. Stay put, please."

This was the break Andi had been waiting for. As soon as he was out the door, she got busy. Just in case that there was a hidden camera installed in the room, she ran over to the armoire and tentatively stretched out her hand toward a beer bottle and quickly pulled it back as if she was fighting the temptation. Then, in a flash, she sat in Doc's chair and familiarized herself with the keyboard of his computer.

She first had to get out of the program that Doc was currently working on - - it appeared to be some sort of medical formula - - then found the Yahoo page and clicked "mail" and then punched in her ID and password. There were three unread messages in her inbox. One of them was from her boss, and it read: *In case you can access this, just letting you know that I'm coming! Hang in there, R. A. Huber.*

Before Andi had a chance to type a response, she heard the door being opened and promptly deleted Huber's e-mail message. Then she hurried around the desk to her own seat. She was sure that the doctor had seen her and therefore was caught.

He said, "What were you doing?"

"I didn't trust myself alone with the bottles, so I checked what you have written in my file," she replied.

He glanced at the computer and raised an eyebrow, asking, "On Yahoo?"

She put forth her best pout and countered, "So what if I checked my e-mail account; after all, I'm not allowed to have my own computer in this place."

"I like that answer better. Always stick with the truth, Andi! And now let's continue the therapy session."

Chapter 33

Mr. White's charm was not lost on R. A. Huber when she interviewed him in his office on that afternoon. The man radiated enthusiasm about Revamp Camp, and his pitch was convincing. Huber imagined that any parent would happily leave a troubled teen in his care. She took notes as he told her all about the young people's daily routine of therapy, schooling, chores, and so forth.

As for the domestic part, he explained that meats and dairy products were being delivered to the facility and that soap, detergents and paper-good items were purchased wholesale. With ample pride he stated that the camp was self sufficient when it came to produce and that they took the surplus to the farmers market in Solvang on Wednesday afternoons. He informed her that the physical work of tending to the crops was of great therapeutic value to the youngsters. Then he went on to describe the chores in the fields with so much eagerness, that, while listening to him, Huber wished she was a farmer. Mr. White also stressed how important it was for each camper to get involved with a hobby or sport.

He stated "We keep them so busy that they have little time or energy for mischief, but drop into bed tired every night."

Huber said, "You mentioned that you're taking the extra produce to market on Wednesday; that would be today, correct?"

He smiled and replied, "I can see where your journalistic eye for detail comes into play. Yes, we'll leave soon. The old pickup truck is already loaded. You probably noticed it in the parking area outside the camp."

She nodded.

"I usually choose a camper to come along with me to Solvang to sell the surplus crop. Our organic produce is in great demand and we seldom have to bring any of it back."

"How do you decide which youngster to take along on that errand?"

"It is a privilege, and the camper that I pick has to be in good standing."

"Which means?"

"No discipline problems for at least two weeks. I'm taking Tyler today, a long-time camper."

Then he explained rules and visiting, or rather, non-visiting policies. All this was old hat to her, since Peter had learned as much from Roger Hawk, but she feigned interest.

When he came to a halt, she inquired, "What kinds of trouble are the juvenile delinquents generally in when they're placed in your charge?"

"All sorts. Most, but not all, are substance abusers of various degrees, be it drugs, alcohol, or both. This may have led them to criminal behaviors, like stealing, dealing drugs, driving under the influence, et cetera. Some are emotionally unstable and suicidal. By the way, I do not like the term 'juvenile delinquents.' They are patients and here to get treatment for their illness, but I prefer to call them campers."

She nodded and then said, "Do you mainly get your campers through referrals from Social Services and Juvenile Hall?"

"No, in most cases it is parents seeking help for their kids that contact us. We are a private undertaking."

"And expensive, I imagine," she said, with a smile.

"Naturally, a place like ours costs money to run."

Then Huber said, "May I ask what prompted you to open the facility?"

Seeing him hesitate, she added, "No need to answer if this is too personal."

After a pause he said, "It *is* personal, but I'll tell you if you'll keep it off the record."

"Absolutely," she replied, and closed her notebook.

"When we were teens, my twin brother overdosed on LSD and had a 'bad trip.' He jumped to his death from a five-story building. I swore right then and there to devote my life to saving others from similar fates."

And before Huber could comment, he changed the subject. Pointing to the large professional-looking camera she carried on a shoulder strap, he said, "What kind of pictures are you planning to take?"

"Oh, whatever looks interesting. Structures, classrooms, fields, and if you don't mind posing, maybe one of you. The paper will only print one or two of the shots, but I like to have an abundance of pictures to choose from."

He said, "I was thinking of the campers. Because most of them are minors, you cannot photograph them without parent permission. We don't want to take the chance of any lawsuits."

"We certainly don't. Rest assured; I will not take any youngster's picture."

Holding her glance with his intense gray eyes, he questioned, "So what else are you planning to do besides taking pictures?"

"I would like to interview some of your staff and a few campers, if I may."

"You have my permission, as long as you don't interfere with our daily routine or interrupt any classes."

"I'll be at my most inconspicuous," she replied, smiling again.

He got to his feet, saying, "Let me show you the property."

Chapter 34

The pupils in Mr. Gilmore's class were laboring over math tests while their teacher sat behind his desk at the head of the classroom playing with his Nintendo DS. Bob Gilmore had lost interest in the students at Revamp Camp some time ago. In his opinion, most were lucky if they finished high school, and only a few would ever see the inside of a university.

He looked up from his game and glanced at the kids who were struggling with the test. Some had the attention span of a toddler. They're a bunch of losers, he thought disgustedly. Then he reconsidered and mused, who am I to judge them? I'm a loser myself!

A few years ago, the young educator with classic Roman good looks had been enthusiastically teaching advanced math and science at a prep school. At that time, he had treated his position not just as a job, but a vocation. Seeing his students hunger for knowledge and being able to satisfy their need had been more than enough compensation for the long hours he had spent preparing the lessons. Life had been good, until the day he took advantage of a student who had a crush on him.

He thought, I've paid dearly for my mistake. The girl was not even a minor; she had been eighteen and practically forced herself on me. Still, what happened was my fault. Now I have to be grateful that the Whiz has given me a second chance with this job. Face it, dude, you're only working for the paycheck and your heart isn't in it, he reproached himself. He wondered for how much longer he would be able to tolerate these miserable kids. At least he was going home at the end of the day. If he were to live here like the rest of the staff, he'd suffocate in this prison.

Glancing out the window pulled him out of his reverie. There was a woman snapping pictures of the school building, and her camera lens seemed to be focused on him. He wondered what was going on out there. Then his expression turned to amusement when he pictured Roberta Ralston next door, taking cover under her desk to avoid being photographed.

Chapter 35

Huber watched the ongoing drill as she strolled by the baseball field. The coach seemed to have the kids under tight control, but, as far as she could tell, they needed lots more practice. An African-American camper, carrying a huge basket, came along the path and stopped next to her. He glanced at the practicing players and shook his head.

She said, "You don't like baseball?"

"Sure I do."

"What's your name?"

"I'm Dewayne, and you're the reporter."

"That's right. So tell me, Dewayne, since you like the sport, how come you're not on the team?"

"Got myself suspended." Then he said, "I can't hang here; gotta get going."

"Where to?"

He pointed to his basket and replied, "Got orders to pick ripe tomatoes."

Huber asked, "May I walk with you? I was planning to take some shots of the crops."

He shrugged and said, "Guess so, if you can keep up."

Dewayne was walking briskly and assumed that his companion would not be able to match his pace; after all, she was an old lady. He soon learned that not only could she keep up, but she felt comfortable enough with his marching tempo to ask questions.

She said, "Have you adjusted to life at Revamp Camp?"

He shrugged again and answered, "I'm alive."

"I can see that, but I don't understand why you made that statement."

"Simple. On the outside, I was always on the lookout; life is cheap on the streets. Here, I only have to watch my back for one person."

"Were you involved with gangs?"

"Uh-huh."

"So you feel safer inside these walls?"

He nodded and said, "Haven't seen anybody carry a weapon."

"Who are you afraid of at camp?"

"I'm scared of nobody and nothing!"

"Whom were you talking about when you said that you had to watch your back for one person?"

"It's not important."

He clearly was not going to say more, so they walked in silence until reaching the tomato plants, where they parted ways. Dewayne got to work, and R. A. Huber continued her farmland exploration. Striding away from the tomato field, she reflected on the people she had talked to so far.

When first admitted inside the facility, she had had an amiable chat with Doreen White. The dainty lady seemed pleased to talk to her and mentioned the term "good press" more than once. With some embarrassment, Mrs. White had admitted to being unfamiliar with the Spy Gazette, so she had emphasized that the paper was a brand-new publication and that they prided themselves on doing human interest stories. The mistress of Revamp Camp was apologetic when enforcing the rules, and Huber smiled to herself as she now recalled part of their dialogue.

Mrs. White had said, "I'm awfully sorry, but I need to search your purse before you can proceed."

Relieved that she'd left her pistol in the glove compartment of her car, she'd replied, "Go ahead if you must, but I don't see why."

The other rummaged through her bag, saying, "I don't like to do this, but I have to follow the rules."

"I can understand searching the youngsters' possessions, but what offensive items could I possibly carry?"

"I know this doesn't apply to you, but you'd be surprised of what some well-meaning parents try to smuggle into camp on visiting day. My husband is strict about this rule; even delivery personnel are made accountable for each object they bring in."

The only forbidden item in the purse had been her cell phone, which Mrs. White was holding onto until the end of the visit.

Then she thought about her encounter with James White. The man was interesting, to say the least. Following the interview in his office and the tour of the building, he had held a brief meeting in the assembly hall to introduce her to the campers. He had ordered them to cooperate if she asked any questions. When he led her to the podium, she had immediately glimpsed the copper-haired young woman in the audience, and when their eyes met, her assistant showed no sign of recognition. She was so proud of Andi.

While chatting with Kyle Norton, the sports coach, the three blasting sounds about knocked her over. She had heard the horn tooting before when it sounded to gather the young people into the assembly hall, but the loud and unexpected noise made her flinch again. The coach had cut the interview short, explaining that three toots meant that school was out and that he needed to head over to the baseball field.

The interviews with the doctor and the one with the matron had also been brief. She had tried hard not to stare at Doc Morrison's ears while talking with him. Although polite, he made it clear that he would not discuss any aspect of the campers' treatments or therapy sessions, as he was bound by doctor/patient confidentiality. He seemed enthusiastic about the research that he conducted in his lab and his eyes gleamed fanatically when he shared that he was on the brink of discovering a drug that would effectively treat cocaine and crack abusers. Ms. Sotto was clearly not the talkative kind and had kept her answers curt. She apparently liked working for Mr. White and found being in charge of the girl campers fulfilling.

Huber was contemplating that it would be hard to figure out what made the matron tick, when she came upon two long rows of green bean stalks. A camper stood at the edge of the first row, picking the firm, crisp and fully elongated pods. As she came closer, he straightened and looked her way. He had a round baby face, but the stare from his eyes was hard and appraising.

She said, "Hi there. I'm R. A. Huber."

"I know."

"And what's your name?"

"It's Mike." And with an unpleasant grin, he remarked, "So the Whiz is doing a publicity stunt; what a gag!"

"What do you mean by that?"

"It's hilarious, that's all."

Huber eyed him expectantly, but he did not explain the outburst and resumed picking beans.

She asked, "Do you like the camp life and field work?"

"No, but I hardly have a choice in the matter."

He was wearing a tank top on this hot day, exposing a nicotine patch tacked to his upper arm. She pointed to it and said, "Stick with it!"

"Easy for you to say," he replied.

"I've been there, and am now smoke free for three-and-a-half years. Believe me, the end result of quitting is well worth the agony you're going through right now."

Pouting, he said, "I'm forced to quit and to wearing the patch. Want to know what I'll do after I'm released from this hard labor camp?" And without waiting for an answer, he continued, "I'll light a cigarette as soon as I'm on the other side of the wall!"

"Let's hope you'll change your mind when the time comes." And she added, "When will that be?"

"What?"

"Do you have an idea when you'll be released?"

"As soon as they think it's safe to let me out, or the sponsors stop funding my guinea pig project, whatever comes first," he said with a bitter sneer.

Huber was ready to move on and, ignoring his snide remark, said, "I wish you all the best for your future."

She had already walked a few steps away when he called after her, "Hey lady! Do you have the exact time?"

Checking her wristwatch she replied, "It is 4:07."

"Already! Time to quit, then, and hike back. I have a therapy session at 4:30."

Chapter 36

With true journalistic flair, R. A. Huber was poised on the path connecting the upper and lower dirt road of the compound, snapping pictures of citrus trees. Her efforts at playing the role went unnoticed, since she was the only human being in that section of the fields. She was about to turn back to the main pathway, when she heard the familiar sound of Andi's Harley-Davidson. Seconds later, she saw her assistant riding toward her, leaving a dust cloud behind.

Andi stopped next to her employer, then looked in all directions and, seeing that the coast was clear said, "Cool camera you've got there, Mrs. Huber!"

"It's a Nikon D-SLR; I'm lucky to have a photographer friend who let me borrow it."

Then she became serious and said, "Glad to see you're all right. I was worried!"

"Sorry boss, but I didn't get a chance to send you any e-mails or reply to yours."

"So you *did* see it!"

"Saw it this mornin'. By a fluke, too. Computers are tight at the camp, and I doubt that I'll get another chance at using one."

"I suspected as much."

Andi remarked, "Sure was a lot easier the time you sent me to Optimum House under cover where I could report to you by phone."

"True, but I can understand why any kind of contact with the outside world is forbidden to the kids at this facility. It makes perfect sense that they need to be removed from their former way of life in order to get rehabilitated. It would not do to let them talk, text message, send e-mails, post on blogs or Twitter and Facebook, or keep in touch in any other way with their old friends."

"I reckon you're right."

With a knowing nod, Huber said, "What a coincidence that I should run into you on this vast estate!"

"You guessed it, boss! I hustled like mad with cleaning Mr. Gilmore's classroom and then came looking for you!"

Then Huber stated, "Okay, let's get down to business; we don't know how much time we've got alone. So far, I've talked with Mr. and Mrs. White, the doctor, the matron and the coach. I've also had chats with a couple of youths I met out here on the property. First I talked with Dewayne and then I ran into a young man named Mike. On the surface, all appears in order at Revamp Camp. Mr. White seems to succeed with turning his juvenile delinquents - - pardon me, his campers - - into responsible members of society."

She thought about the scene in the assembly hall when the young people had all shouted "Yes, Whiz!" in reply to his command. And just a few minutes ago, Mike had also used that word.

She asked, "What's this 'Whiz' business all about?"

"That's what we call Mr. White, and he seems to like it."

Then Huber said, "Now tell me your impressions and whether you have discovered anything dubious about the place. But first off, what about Emily?"

Andi replied, "I've only met her yesterday. Of course I saw her before, but didn't know who she was."

"How is she?"

"Something's wrong with that girl. I have no idea what or why, but she's somewhere else, if you know what I mean."

"Did you talk to her?"

"Yeah, I was the one who did *all* the talkin'."

Huber nodded and then said, "Emily's dad finally reached her by phone, but she was unresponsive with him too. So what gives? Do you think that she has retreated into her own world because of an emotional instability, or do you feel that there is something going on at the camp that triggered her behavior?"

"I don't know. At times I'm convinced that there are evil doings 'round here; at others, I tell myself that it's all in my mind and that I have no real cause for suspicion."

"Is Emily's case an isolated one, or have you noticed others with similar problems?"

Andi thought about it and then said, "The kids all have issues, of course, or they wouldn't be here. I'll tell you what I've learned and you can judge for yourself."

So she told Huber everything, starting with the whispering words between Mona and Tracy that she had overheard, to Tyler's disclosures - - whether real or imaginary - - and ending with Mike's attack.

Huber listened carefully, and then asked, "What do you make of the tête-à-tête you overheard between Mona and Tracy?"

"I keep thinking about it, but haven't figured it out."

"Do you have any idea of what they meant by 'killing the beast'? Is it possible that they are contemplating murder?"

"I questioned Mona, and according to her, what they whispered that night was all pretend and make-believe."

"Do you think she leveled with you?"

Andi exclaimed, "I wish I knew! They mentioned that Emily was cracking up, and now that I've seen Emily close-up, I tend to agree. So here is what I think, but I may be wrong: Something is going on at camp that involves Emily, Mona, Tracy and possibly other inmates too. Whatever it is causes the girls to despair and they resort to the childish idea of planning a mock killing. In other words, it's wishful thinking."

"Let's hope that's all there is to it. Any idea who 'the beast' could be?"

"A couple, but I'd rather not say since it's just a hunch."

Huber laughed and remarked, "I can see that I've taught you well!" Then she became somber as she said, "I'm awfully sorry about Mike's attempted attack on you."

"I came to no harm, and I betcha he's got a new attitude about hitting on women."

"That boy carries a huge chip on his shoulder!" And she asked, "What about Tyler with his active imagination? Have you sorted out facts from fiction regarding his wild stories?"

"I'm tryin' to. It's for sure he makes stuff up, but I'm positive there's some truth in what he said."

"What do you think he meant by telling you that the Whiz has supernatural powers?"

Andi replied, "I don't know about supernatural, but he sure has some kind of power over most of the kids."

"Explain that to me."

"I've noticed that they were awestruck by the Whiz during his pep talk, hanging on his every word."

"What pep talk?"

"Every Monday he gives an inspiring speech in the assembly hall."

"What did he say?"

"I can't remember, but the inmates were mesmerized."

Huber remarked, "Funny, the Whiz calls them campers, you tag them as inmates, I tend to think of them as juvenile delinquents, but they are basically just lost kids." She continued, "Mr. White has lots of charisma; even I felt his charm. I would imagine that inspiring and influencing young people comes easily to him, which seems a good thing given his position as head of this place."

"I think it's more than that."

"Meaning?"

"He has most of them under some kind of a spell."

"Really? Like mass hysteria?"

"Close to."

Her employer inquired, "Were you affected?"

"No, and I'm pretty sure that Mike and Dewayne are immune too."

"Those are the only two young men I met, and they are not under the Whiz's spell. That's interesting!"

Andi suddenly glanced behind them and burst out, "Holy Krewe! Here he comes."

She waited until the Whiz was close enough to hear her and said, "Well, ma'am, nice talkin' with ya. I'd better head back and get cleaned up before supper," and rode off.

Catching up with Huber, the Whiz called out, "There you are! I thought you had gotten lost on our property."

She pointed to the retreating figure on the Harley and said, "I just had a chat with that interesting young woman. I'm surprised you allow her to ride a motorcycle at the camp."

He said, "She's a bit older than our average camper and more responsible. And since she's neither aggressive nor suicidal, I decided that there is no harm in letting her ride."

Huber asked, "How did you do at the farmers market?"

He proudly stated, "As always, our produce was a hit. We sold out in a little over an hour." Then he said, "It's getting late; let me walk you back."

His stride was even faster than Dewayne's had been, and she was almost jogging to keep up with him. The Whiz seemed oblivious of her effort, apparently absorbed in his own train of thought.

Minutes later, the path led slightly uphill and he asked, "Are you done with photographing the crops?"

Catching her breath, Huber said, "Yes, I am. They certainly are impressive. Thank you for giving me free hand at exploring the grounds." And panting now, she added, "I'd like to interview the teachers and a few more campers. May I come back tomorrow?"

Finally aware of his pace, the Whiz slowed down and replied, "By all means!"

Chapter 37

Huber found lodging at a charming Inn on Mission Drive in Solvang, and after checking in, she made a quick call home.

"Hi Peter, it's me."

"Are you on your way back?"

"No, I need more time to sort things out. I'm spending the night in Solvang."

"Did you get a chance to talk with Andi?"

"I certainly did and am happy to report that she's okay and riding around on her motorcycle!"

"See, you worried for nothing!"

"I wouldn't say that. Although Revamp Camp appears in perfect order on the surface, I'm afraid that things are not what they seem."

"Did you meet Emily?"

"Not yet, but I understand that the girl does not act normal." And she related what she had learned from Andi.

Peter said, "Sounds like Emily has completely distanced herself from her surroundings. Whatever triggered this may be too hard for her to handle."

"I agree."

"I'll hold off with telling Roger until we know more."
Then he asked, "Can you wrap this up by tomorrow so I
can expect you home for dinner?"

"I hope so."

"I don't like the idea of spending the evening of our
anniversary alone."

"Me neither!"

After a bit of freshening up and reapplying her lipstick,
Huber joined the tourists who ambled around the Solvang
village. She strolled along Atterdag Road to the Bethania
Lutheran Church on Laurel Avenue and back. Regrettably,
the Hans Christian Andersen Museum on Mission Drive
had already closed. On the corner of Copenhagen Drive
and First Street, the last of the farmers market vendors
were dismantling their booths and loading unsold
produce back onto their trucks. Huber did some window
shopping on Copenhagen Drive and then walked down
Second Street, ending up at the Elverhój Museum, which
was also no longer open that late in the day.

Back on Mission Drive, she found a quaint little place
for dinner and ordered halibut.

Chapter 38

When R. A. Huber returned to Revamp Camp on Thursday morning, she knew right away that something was wrong.

Announcing herself by ringing the bell and gazing into the camera above the entrance gate, she heard Doreen White exclaiming through the intercom, "Oh, Mrs. Huber, I forgot all about you!"

Once Huber had gained access to the building, it was clear that the petite brunette was flustered, saying, "I don't know what to do! I can't disturb my husband right now, and he didn't tell me how to handle you under the circumstances."

Huber said, "What happened?"

"Oh, of course; you don't know. One of our campers had a fatal accident last night."

Huber felt her heart pounding and she forced her voice to stay steady as she asked, "Which camper?"

"His name is Mike."

Dizzy with relief to hear that it was not Andi and feeling grateful to be ushered into a chair since her knees were shaking, Huber said, "I'm so sorry. I chatted with the young man yesterday. Please tell me what happened to him."

Mrs. White repeated, "I just don't know what to do where you're concerned."

Huber gave her an encouraging nod and kept her fingers crossed. The way things stood, she was lucky the mistress of Revamp Camp had admitted her to the premises to begin with; now she might tell her that she was not authorized to disclose details of the accident. On the plus side, the lady had been extremely friendly yesterday and had seemed eager to establish a good rapport with someone representing a newspaper.

Doreen was processing her own reasoning and thought, the press will learn about it sooner or later, so what's the harm in telling her? Screw James! I'm not going to wait for his orders.

Aloud she said, "Mike died of nicotine poisoning."

"That's horrible!" And after a pause she added, "I noticed that he was wearing a nicotine patch."

"That's right; he was on course to quit smoking. Somehow he got hold of a pack of cigarettes and chain-smoked the entire pack while also wearing the patch. We called 911 right away when we found him and the paramedics got here on the double, but too late to revive him."

"Did someone see him smoking?"

"No, but there were cigarette butts scattered all around."

"Didn't he know that smoking and wearing the patch don't mix?"

"Of course he was warned and knew the danger, but apparently Mike was a rebel and tended to swim against the stream." She sighed and continued, "My husband is talking to his people right now."

"They must be devastated by their son's tragic death."

"Oh, you misunderstand. He's not talking with the parents; Mike's an orphan. The meeting is with people from Social Services. The boy is - - I mean was - - in a trial program launched by that department."

Huber seemed to have had a calming effect on Mrs. White, but now, as the sound of footsteps echoed in the corridor followed by a man and a woman entering her office, she became unsettled again and whispered, "That's them."

Huber got to her feet and said, "I'll give you some privacy with these people. Where's the restroom?"

"First door to your left."

The pair ignored Huber as she wandered past them into the hallway and addressed the lady seated at the desk, "We're done here for the moment, but the matter is far from being finalized. We'll be in touch."

That said, they marched out of the administration office in the direction of the front entrance. Doreen was going to chase after them with a friendly peace-offering of coffee or some other beverage, but then thought better of it and pressed the gate button to let them out.

Chapter 39

As the social workers left his office, the Whiz stared at the closing door and thought, what a mess this is turning out to be. Initially, he had been relieved at not having to deal with grieving parents, but these people were relentless. They wanted to know how Mike got his hands on a pack of cigarettes and wouldn't rest until they had the answer. They also kept harping on the idea that the kid might have purposely taken his own life, even though Doc had confirmed that he was not suicidal. The idea of Mike committing suicide was utter nonsense; he was way too cocky and proud of himself.

In a way he could understand their concern since they needed to justify Mike's accident to the sponsors of the program. Not only could the patrons withhold the funds for this particular project if not satisfied, but they could easily stop the money flow for future undertakings.

The Whiz continued his musing, they'll be back after we have the results of the autopsy, and I sure hope that will be the end of it. There is no doubt in my mind that the findings will show that Mike's death was accidental.

He jumped as the ringing of the phone interrupted his train of thought.

"What now?" he hissed.

"Don't get testy with me!" came the agitated reply from his wife. "What do you want me to do with the reporter lady?"

"Oh crud, I forgot that she was coming back today. Send her away." And he quickly changed his mind and said, "No, strike that. I want to talk to her; have her come to my office."

"As soon as I find her."

"Isn't she with you?"

"She stepped out and I don't think she's in the building any longer."

"Great! She's roaming around interviewing staff and campers about Mike's accident. That's all we need, getting the press involved. Hurry up and find her."

Chapter 40

Ms. Ralston faced her English class and said, "I agree with Mr. White and feel it is best for all of us to continue with our normal daily routine. Today's lesson is about synonyms, homonyms and antonyms. After we analyze and discuss these in an extensive manner, I'm confident that every last one of you will never again confuse the terms. So let's ..."

Tyler stopped listening and retreated into a world of his own, thinking back to the previous day. He had accumulated new discoveries and added them to his collection of secrets about people. At the farmers market the Whiz had sent him to get aebleskivers, a sort of pancake puffs, from the bakery across the street. To his great surprise, he saw Mrs. White and another lady sitting at one of the small tables set up for tourists to nibble on their favorite Danish pastries. He had overheard fragments of their conversation about adoption procedures before she noticed him standing nearby, waiting for his order. He remembered the panicked look on her face as she recognized him and then stood up and came closer to him, whispering, "Don't tell the Whiz; it's a surprise."

As for the Whiz, he seemed to have gone on an errand of his own, and rushed back to their booth just as Tyler came out of the bakery.

His session with Doc Morrison had been moved to a later time yesterday because of his trip to the market. As he was waiting his turn outside of the Doc's office, he knew that his therapy session would be cut short and he'd get out on hearing the dinner horn blasts. Mike had ambled by and when passing him had taken a pack of cigarettes out of his pocket. Flashing it before Tyler's eyes, he said, "Look what a little blackmail can do for you!" And with a nasty grin he added, "And I'll get in on the action too."

Now he was reflecting on whom Mike might have been blackmailing. Was it the matron, and her pay-off had been sharing her cigarettes? Or had he found out about Mrs. White's adoption business that she wanted to keep quiet? Could he have learned of the Doc's rats, or discovered the reason for Ms. Ralston's hideout at camp? Maybe there was even a darker side than he already knew to the coach and to Mr. Gilmore. What about if Mike had uncovered a well-kept secret about the Whiz? Tyler couldn't imagine that anyone would have the nerve to blackmail the Whiz, not even Mike. And blackmail for what? He would have to think about this and try to find out more. And then there were the campers. The possibilities of motives for blackmailing staff and campers were endless. He would have to toss the bait and see who'd bite. Tyler rubbed his hands in delight with the prospect of exposing a new dark secret.

"... So can anyone give me an example of synonyms. How about you, Tyler?"

Abruptly forced from his daydreaming, he stuttered, "Blackmailer, extortionist, racketeer."

Ms. Ralston thought, leave it to Tyler to come up with those kinds of words!

Aloud she said, "Good example."

Chapter 41

The night before, disturbing news and gossip about Mike had spread in the girls' dormitory like wildfire. It was hours past the lights-out tooting when Mike's body was driven away by ambulance. The matron had ordered that everyone calm down and go back to bed, and Andi had spent another night tossing and turning.

In the morning, right after breakfast, four horn blasts commanded all campers to gather in the assembly hall where the Whiz told them officially about Mike's accident. Then Andi's therapy session with Doc was interrupted because the Social Services people wanted to speak with him.

Andi's chore assignment for Thursday was cleaning the bathrooms in the school building. She was about to begin that task when Mrs. White walked briskly down the hallway and, after a knock, pulled the door open to Ms. Ralston's classroom.

Andi overheard her addressing the class, "Excuse me for interrupting, but has anyone seen the journalist?"

She got no response and said, "Never mind, then. Carry on," and closed the door again.

As she passed by, Andi stepped out of the bathroom and volunteered, "I haven't seen the lady, but figure she's out snapping more pictures in the fields. Want me to go lookin' for her on my bike?"

"Good idea. When you find her, send her immediately to the Whiz's office."

"Yes, ma'am."

Andi smiled as she got the Harley and donned her gear, thinking, I'll do anything to get out of latrine duty!

Chapter 42

R. A. Huber purposely took the trail connecting the upper to the lower camp road and walked toward the spot where she had run into Andi on the previous day, hoping that her assistant would have the same idea. Before long, she heard the sound of the Harley, this time coming at her from the rear.

She turned her head as Andi rode up next to her and joked, "We have to stop meeting like this!"

Andi killed the engine and returned the banter, "And I knew exactly where to find you too!"

Then Huber became serious and said, "Mrs. White hit me with the news of Mike's death. Now tell me what you know about it."

"Not as much as I'd like to, boss. Late last night, one of the girls came running into the dorm telling us that someone from the search party looking for Mike had found him, and that he was dead. I didn't even know that he'd been missing! After that, there was lots of speculation and gossiping going 'round, and this mornin', I've talked to a couple of inmates who seem to know more than what the Whiz told us in the assembly hall.

"Here is what I've pieced together so far: Mike didn't show up at the eatery for dinner. Nobody was too concerned at the time, as he had bragged to another camper that he had better things to do. He told that camper to inform the Whiz that he felt sick and was going to bed. Much later, the coach noticed that Mike wasn't in the boys' dormitory. When he couldn't be found anywhere in the main building, study hall or school, the Whiz and coach organized an outdoor search party equipping everyone with flashlights."

Huber asked, "Do you know who was in the search party?"

"I think it was all guys; the Whiz, the coach, and all the boy campers."

"What about the doctor and math teacher?"

"They don't live at camp and had long gone home."

"Sorry for the interruption. I just wanted to be clear on who went on the search. It's probably of no importance. Please go on."

"Anyhow, they didn't have to go far until they found him by the tool shed, which is a short distance from the baseball field."

"I know exactly where it is; I walked by it on my way to the farmland. Who found him?"

"It was Brandon and Dewayne. The search team went in pairs."

"Did you speak with the two boys today?"

"I only talked to Brandon. He's shy, and I had to drag every word out of him. At first they thought that Mike had just passed out, but then Brandon touched his hand, and according to him, it was stone cold and lifeless. They alerted the others and then the Whiz called 911. Oh, Brandon also said that they shined their flashlights on a bunch of cigarette butts scattered in the area around Mike. And that's about all I learned from him."

"What's your personal opinion on Mike's accident?"

"Well boss, I've been thinking about it non-stop. My first reaction was that most likely we're not dealing with an accident. But then I figured, if he died of nicotine poisoning, how can it be anything else? Mike is not the suicidal kind, and you can hardly force someone to smoke himself to death while wearing the nicotine patch, now can you?"

"Good point! I presume that they're doing an autopsy, so at the moment we don't know the cause of death for sure."

"Guess not."

"What are your other ideas on the matter?"

Andi replied, "Mike *was* my prime suspect as being 'the beast.'"

The emphasis on the word "was" caught Huber's attention and she asked, "And now he no longer is?"

"Last night in the dorm when I first heard about Mike, I tackled Mona by saying, 'Your wish came true!' She didn't seem to understand, so I went on, 'The beast is gone now.' She stared at me, not seeming to take it in, then her eyes got as big as saucers and she yelled, 'Oh my God! I know now what you're thinking and you're dead wrong.'"

"You think she's on the level and Mike was not the person she and her friend talked about the night you overheard their conversation?"

"You should have seen Mona's face, boss. She was shocked and appalled at the idea."

"So we're back to the drawing board."

Andi nodded and said, "I wish you could stay and help me figure things out, but I'm sure the Whiz isn't keen on having anyone from the press hanging 'round now. Publicity about a kid dying at his camp, accident or not, can't be good advertising for him."

"True, but I'm working on an idea to convince him that it might be to his advantage to stick with me."

"That reminds me, he's in a big hurry to see you!"

"I had better walk back, then."

Andi turned the bike around, then untied the extra headgear attached to the back of her saddle, and holding it out to her boss, said, "I came prepared to give you a ride; so here's Daddy's helmet. Hop on."

Huber strapped the helmet on, and while swinging one leg behind Andi over the saddle asked, "Are you allowed to take passengers?"

Andi grinned and replied, "No, the Whiz strictly forbade it, but hey, I'm a juvenile delinquent!"

Then she took off with a jerk, making her employer grab onto her waist for dear life.

Chapter 43

The Whiz came straight to the point and said, "In dealing with the current situation, I insist that your paper - - what's the name of it again?"

Huber said, "Spy Gazette."

"Right. I insist that the Spy Gazette does not print anything about the accident, and you might as well know that I regret having agreed to your writing an article about Revamp Camp."

"I understand your concern and will honor your wish for discretion about the accident. On the other hand, some positive advertising for your facility can't hurt."

He did not answer and seemed preoccupied with his own thoughts, so Huber waited.

When the silence became awkward, he suddenly asked, "Do you smoke?"

"Not any longer; I quit years ago."

"I'm trying to figure out how Mike got that pack of cigarettes."

"And you think that I gave it to him? That's a bit farfetched!"

"My idea was that he might have seen you smoke and bummed the cigarettes off you. I know that I'm grasping at straws, but I can't imagine how he managed to get hold of the pack."

"I see your point now."

He continued, "Mike had no visitors on the previous weekend, and even if he had been able to convince some other kid's parent to smuggle cigarettes into camp, I doubt that he would have waited four days before smoking them. At the farmers market yesterday, Tyler was never out of my sight except for the short time when I sent him to the bakery to get aebleskivers, and he brought me back the exact change."

"I'm not sure that I understand what you mean about the exact change?"

"Campers don't have their own money while they're here. Since he gave me back the correct change from the purchase in the bakery, he obviously did not have any money to buy a pack of cigarettes for Mike."

"I understand now."

"Other than you and the staff, no one was admitted to the camp in the last few days."

Eyeing him keenly, Huber asked, "All the staff members are above suspicion?"

He held her glance and replied, "Absolutely!"

"By the way, is it established that Mike smoked the entire pack?"

"Almost; there were two cigarettes left inside the pack that was found in his pocket."

"Is it crucial for you to find out who supplied the young man with cigarettes?"

"Of course it is!"

She said, "Setting the Spy Gazette aside, I personally could be of value to you."

"Really?"

"I'm inconspicuous and could keep my eyes and ears open. I'm also trained to ask the right questions to get people to open up. You, on the other hand, attract attention and the kids might clam up."

He mulled it over and then asked, "What's in it for you?"

"Let's just say that the puzzle caught my interest."

The Whiz's piercing gray eyes held hers for a long moment. He was finally satisfied and remarked, "Yes, I believe you're the curious sort." And with a charismatic chuckle he stated, "You're on!"

Chapter 44

Tyler's thought-process that had started in Ms. Ralston's classroom followed him to the math class next door. Unlike the English teacher who had jolted him out of his mental absorption, forcing him back to participate in her lesson, Mr. Gilmore couldn't care less. As was his habit, the math and science teacher ignored the students who did not pay attention, which was about 80% of his class.

So Tyler had free rein to continue his musing. He played back the events of the previous day in his mind's eye, trying to determine whom Mike could have been blackmailing. By resolving who'd dished out the pack of cigarettes, he would have the answer. He tried to remember every detail from the time he got up in the morning to his trip to the farmers market, the search-party for Mike, until the ambulance had driven his body away after lights-out in the dorm.

The picture of Mike flaunting the forbidden cigarettes flashed back at him, and so did the sentence, "I'll get in on the action." At the time, he had shrugged it off as Mike's typical ill-natured bragging. Now he pondered, what action? Suddenly, he knew where the pack had come from. The idea was simple, and he felt surprised that it had not occurred to him right away. Then he took the concept a step further and refocused on the cause for blackmail. And piece by piece, it all started to make sense.

Tyler had never consciously let himself reflect on this before, but everything pointed to the fact that there was wickedness going on at Revamp Camp. And he was sure that it did not start yesterday, but had been brewing for a long time. He could be wrong, of course. Assuming that he was right, it would explain why he wasn't able to function in the outside world any more. It also made him understand why the weekends were such a drag and everything fell back into place came Monday.

As he walked out of Gilmore's classroom, his mind was made up. He would take the bull by the horns and ask some crucial questions.

Chapter 45

R. A. Huber was invited to the noon meal at Revamp Camp. The Whiz had left it up to her to either lunch among the campers in the eatery or join his wife and some of the staff in the small room next to the kitchen. She chose the mess hall.

Now she sat between two young people, nibbled on a tasty quesadilla, and listened to the camper at the lectern read from a book of daily reflections. Soon her attention to the inspiring words faded and her main focus was to observe the folks in the room. The majority of kids were unknown to her with the exception of a few familiar faces. Her place was at the middle table where the Whiz presided, and from where she had a clear view of Andi, who ate at the matron's domain. The young man named Dewayne sitting in the coach's area had his gaze fixed on her, but when their eyes met, he looked away and gulped his lunch.

An ash-blond, blue-eyed camper near the head of her table caught Huber's attention. She looked about fourteen but must have been older. At first, Huber thought that she was transfixed by the words that were being read, but then realized that the young girl was in a stupor. The food in her plate remained untouched, and the way she tilted her head and stared into the distance was unnatural. Then Huber's glance went back to Andi, and her assistant answered the question in her eyes with a barely noticeable nod. So she knew that she had found Emily.

The reader had finished at last, and the sound of the Whiz's baritone filled the room, "Campers, the silence is lifted; you are permitted to talk."

"Thank you, Whiz!" they responded in unison.

As conversations started to flourish throughout the room, the young man sporting a goatee who sat next to Huber turned to her and said, "So the press is still hanging on, that's interesting." Followed by, "And you're sitting in the haunted chair!"

"Don't be morbid, Tyler," remarked the female camper on her other side.

The lady detective caught on right away and said, "Oh, was this Mike's place?"

"You bet, and he's watching."

Then he bent over his plate, apparently oblivious to his surroundings, and kept quiet for the rest of the meal. Huber was fascinated with her table neighbor and hoped that he would open up to her further.

As people started to get up and disperse, the young woman on her other side said, "Don't believe a thing that comes out of Tyler's mouth. He's crazy and nobody takes him seriously." And before Huber could think of a response, the girl walked away.

Soon most had left the table, but Tyler lingered. He briefly glanced over to the space at the head of the table, making sure that it had emptied, and then said, "What do you want to know about macabre Revamp Camp?"

"Whatever you care to contribute."

A nasty little laugh escaped him and he said, "I can picture the headline in your paper: *Extortionist gets his punishment by smoking himself to death!"* He covered his mouth and added, "Oops, that slipped out."

"Mike was a blackmailer?"

"Yep, he told me so himself."

"Whom did he blackmail?"

"Don't know for sure yet."

"Any idea of how he got his hands on a pack of cigarettes?"

"Can't say for a fact either, but talk to me again later and I'll have the answer to both questions."

He got up and had taken a few steps toward the door when Huber called to him, "Young man!"

He turned his head to face her, and she looked at him gravely and stated, "Be careful."

Chapter 46

Huber waited in the hallway as the stream of students came rushing out of Roberta Ralston's classroom. When the last camper had ambled out the door and past her, she entered.

The teacher was erasing history quotations off the blackboard, and Huber's first view of her was from the back. Then she turned around, pallid in alarm.

Huber said, "So sorry, I didn't mean to frighten you." And with an encouraging smile, she continued, "Mr. White might have informed you that someone from Spy Gazette is writing a piece about Revamp Camp; I'm that person."

The scared look remained on Ms. Ralston's face as she said, "Please don't mention me in your paper."

"Don't worry, I won't name anyone. The article will mainly describe camp life. Let me ask you a few questions."

She pointed to a front-row student's desk saying, "Have a seat, then," and hurried to close the classroom door before grabbing a chair for herself, and then joined Huber.

The latter first inquired into general topics about the campers' school routines, which the teacher answered without hesitation. The broad-based questions seemed to put her at ease and she elaborated on the class curriculum.

Watching and listening to the young woman, Huber suddenly realized that she must be lonely. It occurred to her that the meek and mousy Roberta Ralston could be attractive and appealing to the opposite sex if she chose to let her hair down.

Then she asked, "Are you shocked about Mike's accident?"

"Of course!"

"His friends must be devastated."

Ms. Ralston wavered for a second before she stated, "He didn't make friends easily; the majority of kids were afraid of him."

"What kind of a student was he?"

"Mike had a longer attention span than most."

"But didn't apply himself?"

"That's right. He was an angry young man."

Huber agreed, "I had the same impression."

"You knew him?"

"We met in the fields yesterday and chatted briefly. He even commented that he'd smoke the first chance he'd get when released from camp."

Astonished, she asked, "He said that to you?"

"Something to that effect. Do you have any idea who gave him the pack of cigarettes?"

"I haven't got a clue."

There didn't seem anything left to discuss, so R. A. Huber thanked the teacher for her time, got to her feet, and walked toward the door. Suddenly she stood still and then retraced her steps.

"One more thing."

"Yes?"

"Tell me, Ms. Ralston, whom are you hiding from?"

Stunned, she stared at Huber, whose gaze was steady and demanding. Seconds passed in silence as they faced one another.

Roberta finally said, "I'm hiding from my ex."

"Was he abusive?"

"That is putting it mildly. He beat me on a regular basis and threatened to kill me if I ever left him. One day I mustered up the courage to leave and then divorced him. In spite of the restraining order, he came after me with a knife and almost succeeded with his threat."

She opened up the top two buttons of her blouse and exposed a scar that started at her collar bone and extended into her bra area and continued, "I changed my name and came here. So far I've been safe, but deep down I know that he'll find me eventually."

Suddenly embarrassed, she added, "I haven't told a soul about this in the three years I've been teaching here."

Huber said, "It helps to talk about it, though. Three years is a long time; I would wager that you have nothing to fear any longer." And before finally making her exit, she remarked, "It is time for you to start living again."

The lady detective walked out of the school building thinking, at least one mystery is solved. Roberta, for her part, mused, what on earth made me open up to this complete stranger?

Chapter 47

From Bob Gilmore, the math and science teacher, Huber had not learned anything new. He had been pleasant enough but kept his opinion about Mike or camp life in general to himself. When she strolled by the sports field, another baseball practice was in progress and she briefly stopped to watch. She saw no great improvement in the players from the previous day, but this certainly was not for the coach's lack of trying.

Soon, the tool shed came into view and she decided to have a look around. On searching the ground, she found some cigarette butts stumped into the dirt near the tractor and other machinery, but most were lying in clumps by the bench in front of the small structure. Huber pictured Mike sitting on it, taking in his last puffs. Why didn't he stop smoking, or at least take off the patch when he felt ill? she reflected. It had made no sense to her when she first learned about the accident, and it didn't make sense now.

She peeked inside the shed. A couple of ladders and a selection of rakes, shovels, pitchforks and spades of all sizes stood neatly arranged against one wall. Another held a bottom shelf with trimmers, hedge cutters, saws and hoses, and an upper rack was loaded with a large assortment of seeds. At a table in the center, she noticed all kinds of hand gardening tools like shears, clippers, cutters, trowels and weeders, as well as gloves and a compost thermometer. Interesting how so many items could be stored in such a small space, she thought.

Having learned from yesterday's experience that trekking along dirt roads in sandals and shaking out gravel lodged between the sole and bottom of her foot was a nuisance, she came prepared. Now she was clad in sneakers and, feeling the urge for some exercise, started jogging. Without fail, every time she was away from home with no access to the gym or a racquet ball court, the itch for physical activity hit her with a vengeance.

The Galas looked almost ripe to Huber when she scampered by the apple orchards. By the time she got near the vegetable gardens, her breath became labored and she opted to take a break upon reaching the young men whom she had spotted at work from a distance. There were three of them, and the one closest to the trail was Dewayne, who was smoothing dirt with a rake.

When she came to a halt next to him, he looked up from his toil and said mockingly, "Training for the Senior Olympics?"

Still panting, she humored him and replied, "Maybe in future decades. What are you planting?"

"Nothing yet; we're making the soil ready to put in lettuce seeds."

Then she said, "So you're still suspended from baseball."

"Uh-huh, but the Whiz is letting me back tomorrow. About high-time; without me, we can't win against the visiting team."

After a pause she said, "You stared at me during lunch. Is there something you wanted to tell me?"

He interrupted his work and, leaning on his rake, answered, "Nah, just tried to figure out who you are."

"You already know that I'm R. A. Huber from the Spy Gazette."

He looked behind him, making sure that the other kids working the soil were not within earshot and said, "Don't think so! You're spying, but it ain't for any Gazette. You smell like the heat. Which is it; cop or private eye?"

Totally taken aback, Huber blinked. Within seconds, she was in control again and asked, "What gives you that idea?"

"I know a mole when I see one."

"Then what do you think is my purpose here?"

He shrugged and said, "Maybe you're nosing about Mike's death."

"You forget that I arrived at Revamp Camp before his accident."

"And you're still snooping. Can't take that long to put a piece of write-up together!"

Huber stated, "That's where you're wrong, young man. The research for this particular article takes time; there's no guarantee that I'll be able to wrap things up even by tomorrow."

She could see it in his eyes that he started to falter and continued, "As a seasoned journalist, I'm looking at all angles. Tell me, Dewayne, *is* there something about Mike's accident to nose about?"

He checked his surroundings again. The two other campers were still laboring a distance away, but getting closer. Keeping his voice low, he replied, "Mike was a mean SOB, but no idiot."

"So what are you saying?"

"I don't buy the nicotine poisoning stuff."

"What do you suggest?"

"He was wasted."

Huber whispered back, "In what manner and by whom?"

"How should I know? I didn't do it!"

Dewayne got busy with his rake again, and it was clear to Huber that their conversation was over.

Chapter 48

On her jog back from the fields, Huber was already near the school structure when she ran into Mrs. White, who said, "Here you are at last! My husband needs to talk with you."

"Do I find him in his office?"

"Yes, he's waiting."

"Thanks, I'd better hurry up, then."

Oh boy! Huber thought, continuing her jog in the direction of the main building. Does this mean that Dewayne is not the only person who is suspicious of me?

To her surprise, the Whiz did not seem angry at her when she entered his office. He announced, "We have the autopsy results, and knowing how Mike got his pack of cigarettes is not important any longer, even though I aim to find out eventually."

"Are you telling me that he didn't die of nicotine poisoning?"

"He had a substantial amount of nicotine in him, but that wasn't the cause of death. He succumbed to a high insulin overdose."

"Mike was a diabetic?"

"Yes, an insulin-dependent one. Evidently, he skipped dinner and smoked a pack of cigarettes instead. The theory is that his accidental overdose on an empty stomach was too much for his body to handle."

Huber said, "That makes more sense to me than did the nicotine poisoning."

"As I said, there is evidence that he smoked the cigarettes and wore the patch at the same time, but severe hypoglycemia turns out to be the cause of death."

"An amazing coincidence, don't you think?"

The Whiz pinned her with a piercing look and said, "Coincidences do happen."

Then he checked his watch and stated, "I have a few things to take care of before the sounding of the dinner horn. You are welcome to our eatery again, if you like."

"I'd love to. Thank you very much!"

On her way out the door she said, "As you mentioned, there is no longer an urgent need to look into the matter of how Mike got hold of his pack, but I still would like to interview a few more youngsters for my article about Revamp Camp. May I come back tomorrow?"

"I can't think of a reason why you shouldn't," he replied with an engaging grin.

Chapter 49

Tyler was the first to arrive at the rendezvous and started second-guessing the merit of the meeting. Earlier in the day, his challenging accusations had neither been admitted nor denied, and he hadn't questioned the command: "Meet me inside the tool shed before dinner and I'll show you." Now, after spending ten minutes in the claustrophobic place, he doubted that there was anything to discover here. And why the tool shed of all places? His suspicions had nothing to do with gardening implements. On the other hand, he hardly had been given a choice but to follow orders.

Mulling over his speculation for the umpteenth time, he suddenly doubted his own judgment. Was he wrong and the blackmailing was about something entirely different? He would soon find out when he faced the extortionist's victim. Hurry up and get here, I'm dying of curiosity, he thought.

At last he heard the sound of rapidly approaching footsteps, and then the person materialized at the opening of the shed, saying, "Let's get this over with; we don't have much time."

Tyler asked, "So what did Mike have on you?"

"Check out the top rack over there, and find out for yourself!"

Tyler went to the indicated wall and eagerly rummaged around the top shelf for something intriguing. There were several boxes filled with envelopes of any kind of fruit and vegetable seeds imaginable. He searched inside each box for an incriminating article but came up empty-handed.

Exasperated, he said, "I see tons of seeds, but nothing else. What am I missing?"

There was no answer, but at that instant he heard two horn blasts signaling that he had five minutes to get to the eatery for dinner.

Tyler turned around and saw the pitchfork coming at him a split-second too late.

Chapter 50

Immediately after taking possession of her phone and walking out the gate, Huber called home.

"Happy Anniversary, Peter! And I'm awfully sorry."

"So you're not ready to come home yet. Can't say that surprises me."

"I'll have to spend at least another night."

"Guess that means eating dinner at *Chez Tante Jeanne* and celebrating by my lonesome. How about you; are there any gourmet places in Solvang?"

"I already ate in the mess hall."

"So Regula, are you making any progress with your investigation?"

"Not as much as I'd like. Interested?"

"I'm all ears!"

Peter paid keen attention as she walked him through her entire day. When she finally came to a halt, he said, "Bet you're happy that Andi 'runs into you' on her bike and you can huddle without being overheard."

"I only hope our luck keeps up."

Then Peter said, "Did you talk to that Tyler kid later and was he any help?"

"That's just it; I'm worried about him. I was thrilled when the Whiz invited me again for dinner and was sure that I'd be sitting next to Tyler once more so we'd get a chance to chat."

"But you were placed somewhere else?"

"No, Tyler never showed up for dinner."

"And that worries you?"

"Yes, I think something happened to him."

"Come now, Regula, maybe he wasn't hungry and skipped the meal."

"They have strict rules and regulations here. A camper needs to have a good excuse for ignoring the horn call for meals, or any other command for that matter."

"So the kid was missed?"

"Of course. The Whiz's first question as he walked to the head of the table was, 'Where is Tyler?' No one seemed to know, which clearly annoyed him."

Then Peter asked, "Do you think the other kid - - I believe you said his name was Dewayne - - is correct with his suspicion that Mike was murdered?"

"My instinct tells me 'yes,' but according to the autopsy result he died of an insulin overdose, which makes it accidental."

"You can't argue with medical evidence. So what's your game plan?"

Regula stated, "I have to concentrate on the reason Andi and I are here in the first place, which is finding the cause for Emily's apathy."

"Have you talked with Emily?"

"No, and I don't think it makes a difference. I get the picture from Andi's experience with the girl."

"Any idea what's going on in the camp?"

"Not precisely, but I can tell you this much: It is all evil."

"I hope you get to the source of that evil soon. Roger is getting impatient and I'd like to have something concrete to tell him."

Just before they hung up he said, "By the way, I saw a good deal I couldn't resist and booked us a flight to Madrid for October."

"I can hardly wait!"

Chapter 51

The Sheriff's car Huber saw parked in front of the gate as she pulled into the dirt lot on Friday morning confirmed her fear. When she was admitted into the administration office, she found Doreen White in turmoil.

The mistress of Revamp Camp was clearly agitated, and Huber asked, "You have more bad news?"

"That's putting it mildly," she replied. "A tragedy would be more accurate."

"What happened?"

"Tyler was murdered."

The image of the young man leaving the eatery as she had called out her warning to be careful flashed back into Huber's mind.

She said, "I am so sorry." And after a pause, "You are certain that it was a homicide?"

Mrs. White's voice was shaky when she replied, "He was stabbed with a pitchfork. I can't believe there is a killer running loose at our camp!"

"When did it happen?"

"Yesterday evening; he was found all bloody in the tool shed." She shivered and continued, "The police questioned some of us last night and then came back early this morning. Their grilling is still going on as we speak."

Huber nodded. "I saw a Sheriff's car parked up front." Then she had an idea and said, "With a police investigation in progress, they might not trust me with the camera. I had best take it back to my car. Would you kindly let me out and then back inside the gate?"

"Oh, of course," she said, and pressed the gate button.

While walking to her car Huber thought, I'm taking a chance here, and if it doesn't work out, I'll be in trouble. To my advantage, Mrs. White is flustered today, and since she already checked my bag when she first admitted me, she may forget to do it again when I come back.

First she stowed away the camera in the trunk of the car and then stepped inside and took her loaded .25 caliber pistol out of the glove compartment and placed it into her purse. While striding back through the gate, she reasoned that she had a permit for the pistol and a right to carry it. Should it be discovered, the worst case scenario would be that she'd blown her cover.

When she reentered the administration office, Mrs. White spoke into the phone, "Yes sir, I'll send her right over." And to Huber, "Lieutenant Johansson wants to talk with you."

"The Sheriff?"

"Yes, he's using my husband's office for questioning."

"I had better head on over, then," Huber said, sighing with relief as she marched down the hallway.

Chapter 52

At that moment Andi was mopping the hallway in the school building while letting her mind wander, thinking about the previous evening and all that had happened since. She had been doing a puzzle in the hobby room when Jacob came bursting in and announced, "Dewayne found Tyler murdered in the tool shed!" And soon afterwards, four horn blasts had called everyone to the assembly hall, where the Whiz introduced Lieutenant Johansson, who confirmed Jacob's claim.

The lieutenant stated that he was from the Santa Barbara County Sheriff's Department, which provided police services to the Santa Ynez Valley, and that he had command over Solvang and Buellton. He told his audience Tyler's body had already been taken away, but that there were still people working at the crime scene. He asked everyone to remain in the assembly hall until called for questioning. Then, one by one, he interviewed the staff members, except for Doc Morrison and Mr. Gilmore, who had already gone home, followed by the male campers, starting with Dewayne. When it was getting late and Andi began anticipating having to spend the night in the assembly hall, the officer appeared again and adjourned the rest of the interviews to the next day.

Once more, Andi had trouble falling asleep at night. She had liked the funny-looking guy with his wild imagination. Stretched out on her bunk she thought, poor Tyler, you collected one secret too many. I'll avenge you, I swear! And then she applied herself to some serious rehashing of all that she had learned since coming to the camp.

Had she missed something during her first Antabuse treatment and the beer episode? At the time she'd been too sick to give it further thought, but now she debated whether she'd heard noises coming from Doc's lab. Or could it be that she had heard nothing at all and later was influenced by Tyler's story about rats? While spending a good part of that day in misery on the psychiatrist's couch, she'd been oblivious to what went on around her. A vague memory of kids coming and going, presumably for their treatments, flashed back into her mind. She even recalled the Whiz briefly looking in on her to check how she was doing.

Lying awake, Andi had mulled over every conversation she'd had with campers and staff. What was it that Jacob said that time in the music room? She couldn't recall his exact words, but it was something about him being programmed. And he had had a robotic expression on his face as he said, "Everybody likes the Whiz." She visualized the meeting in the assembly hall when the Whiz gave his pep talk. Mike, Dewayne and a few others had not seemed under their leader's spell. What did this handful of campers have in common? she wondered. Maybe there lay the answer.

Not for the first time her brain turned to revisit the long chat she'd had with Tyler in the laundry room when he disclosed some of the dark secrets about people, whether real or imagined. Which of his wild accusations was true? And what is Ratio D?

And then she thought about what she had overheard Mona whispering to Tracy on her first night, "We have to kill the beast." It always came back to who "the beast" was!

Andi had worked her mop and pail halfway down the school building's corridor as she continued her musing. Early in the morning the questioning of the girls began. They were asked to stay in their dormitory and scrub room until called to see the Sheriff. Andi had showered and was sitting on her top bunk when the matron called out that it was Tracy's turn to go down to the Whiz's office. Now she replayed the following exchange of words in her mind:

As Tracy walked by their beds, Mona gave her friend a hard stare and muttered, "Make sure you hold your tongue, girl!"

Andi said, "I heard that!" as soon as Tracy was gone.

Mona ignored her.

With one jump of her long legs Andi hit the floor and then was in Mona's face, saying, "Enough of this cat-and-mouse game! You and I are gonna talk, you hear?"

Mona recoiled and gawked at her, but still didn't answer.

"What's the matter with you? Are you gonna let someone else get killed before you tell what goes on in this place?"

"Keep your voice down," Mona hissed.

Andi struggled to control her anger and said, "Never mind keepin' me quiet. I saw the matron leave; she's probably in the scrub room. As for the girls, they're all zombies anyhow! I want some answers from you. Is that clear?"

There was fear written all over her face, but the plucky girl kept up her tough image and replied, "Depends what you're going to ask."

"First off, who is the beast?"

"Sorry, can't tell you."

"Then give me a clue of what the hell is wrong at Revamp Camp."

After a long pause Mona finally said, "Don't know about the male campers, but aside from a few exceptions - - and it looks like you're one of them - - we girl campers are doomed."

Before Andi got a chance to explore what that meant, she heard the matron calling, "Andi, you're next."

Lieutenant Johansson was a big man in his forties. He had introduced his subordinate as Andi walked into the Whiz's office, but she couldn't remember his name now. The interview had been brief, and she was sure that she didn't add anything new to the information the officers had collected from countless inmates questioned ahead of her. The lieutenant was clearly in charge and after going over her personal data had given her a strange look when learning that she came to the facility of her own accord. Andi wasn't sure if his glance was that of disbelief or admiration.

The routine questions were soon dealt with, like giving an account of her movements of the previous evening and when she'd seen Tyler last. Then he wanted to know how well she had known the victim and what conversations she'd had with him. So she shared a few of his wild tales. When the Sheriff inquired if she believed Tyler's stories, she had replied that obviously one of them must be true since it had backfired. He gave her that same look again and then let her go.

Schedules were mixed up because of the ongoing police investigation, and Andi's therapy session with Doc Morrison was moved to sometime in the afternoon. Still, the Whiz had insisted that classroom activities and everybody's chores would be kept up. Now she had arrived at the end of the hallway, and after wringing out the mop and getting rid of the dirty pail water, she finished her janitorial task with ten minutes to spare before class was let out.

Chapter 53

Meanwhile, R. A. Huber sat in the hot-seat at the Whiz's office.

Her personal information established, Lieutenant Bill Johansson commented, "Regula Agatha Huber; are you German?"

"No, Swiss."

"Ah, Switzerland is a beautiful country." Then he cleared his throat and said, "Now then, Ms. Huber - -

"I prefer Mrs."

"Okay, *Mrs.* Huber, let's get on with it. I understand that you are here in the capacity of a reporter from - - what's the name again?"

"Spy Gazette."

"Right. I'm unfamiliar with that publication."

"It's a fairly new paper."

"So what did Spy Gazette send you here to report?"

"We are doing a segment on solutions for the staggering increase of troubled youth in our society. Revamp Camp is one of several rehabilitation facilities for juveniles that we are researching."

"I see." Then he pinned her with an inquisitive glance and asked, "Are you planning to report on the homicide?"

"No, sir, I have already given Mr. White my word that I will not mention the first tragedy and am planning to keep that promise in the case of the second as well."

"By the first tragedy, you mean the fatal insulin overdose another young man accidentally injected himself with?"

"Yes, that's what I'm referring to."

"You certainly seem to have unfortunate timing!" He turned to his minion seated in the corner and said, "Sergeant, hand me your notes for a sec," and grabbed the sheet of paper.

After going over it, he stated, "You arrived at 2:05 on Wednesday afternoon. On that same night a young man had a lethal accident. You came back yesterday morning, and on that evening another youngster was killed."

Taken by surprise, Huber said, "Are you suggesting that I had something to do with either incident?"

"Not at all! Like I said, it was bad timing."

"And coincidental, I assure you."

Then the lieutenant asked, "Do you have a local accommodation?"

"I'm staying at a hotel in Solvang."

"Please give us the name and address."

Huber took the hotel business card from the outside pocket of her purse and, handing it to him, asked, "So you can check that I left Revamp Camp before the tragic events on both evenings?"

"Just a formality," he replied.

When she left the Whiz's office moments later, she thought, I can't believe he seriously considers me a suspect!

Chapter 54

At lunch, Huber tried to shake the eerie sensation caused by the conspicuously empty seat next to her. She was also aware that the young people around her took great care to avoid glancing at that spot, and when she cast an eye toward the head of the table, she received a shock. Overnight, the Whiz seemed to have aged ten years. Lines of anxiety marked his face, and his charismatic spark was replaced by a worried expression. With a flash of compassion, Huber thought, the man has good reason to worry. Revamp Camp may not be able to sustain murder on its premises. Even if the culprit was eventually brought to justice, it would be hard to lose the stigma.

Just like the day before, Emily sat expressionless, staring into space. So far the girl had not touched the sandwich in her plate. Was she even aware that a murder had been committed? Huber wondered.

Looking over to the matron's table, she failed to get Andi's attention straightaway since the latter appeared to be in deep mental absorption. Finally, their eyes met and Huber made a point of checking the time on her wristwatch and then gave Andi an inquiring stare. At first, her assistant did not catch on, and she had to repeat the maneuver. Presently, Andi unobtrusively held up two fingers and Huber thought, ah, she got it; we meet at two o'clock.

Chapter 55

Huber knew that sooner or later she would be caught. When she was re-summoned to the Whiz's office after lunch, she discovered that it would be sooner.

Lieutenant Johansson stated, "You lied to us, Mrs. Huber! There is no paper by the name of Spy Gazette, and you definitely are no journalist. We've checked you out; you're a private investigator."

"Am I in big trouble for impersonation?"

"You were clever enough to use your own name, so technically you impersonated no one. However, you are here under false pretenses."

"Which still gets me into trouble?"

A cunning smile escaped the lieutenant when he answered, "If you level with us and fully cooperate with our investigation, I might show you leniency. But I want the truth!"

"That is understood," she replied.

"First off, did Mr. White hire you?"

"No, he is unaware of my position."

"Explain the purpose of your business at the camp, then."

Without mentioning a name, Huber said that she was hired by the parent of a resident and also the reason why. When asked what she had delved into in the last two days, she described her interviews with members of the rehabilitation facility and what she had learned from her encounters with staff and juveniles. The lady was fair enough to clue him in on some of her suspicions. She ended by contributing impressions she had formed when talking with the two deceased boys.

The Sheriff heard her out and then asked, "Are you acting alone?"

Huber's first impulse was to say "Yes," in order not to compromise Andi, but then she thought better of it. Lieutenant Johansson was no fool and probably had good reason to ask the question. He might already have checked Andi's background.

So she admitted, "I sent someone to live here under cover."

"Would that be Antoinette LeJeune, originally from New Orleans?"

"You guessed right."

"Have you two been able to consult with one another?"

She smiled and replied, "Yes, thanks to my assistant's hobby of riding a Harley-Davidson!"

"So how's the sleuthing coming?"

Was the man making fun of her, she wondered?

Aloud she answered, "The puzzle pieces are starting to fall into place."

"Are you saying that you've figured out what you came to investigate?"

"If you mean what evil lurks beneath the surface at Revamp Camp, the answer is that we have several ideas."

"Care to share your findings with me and the sergeant?"

"I'd rather not, until we are certain."

"What about the homicide."

"It all hangs together, don't you think?"

"Is there more information you can provide us with?"

"Nothing comes to mind at the moment, sir."

There was an austere glint in his eye when he said, "You make sure you let us know when it does!"

Huber felt herself dismissed, but was not ready to leave yet.

She said, "May I ask you a question?"

"Sure," he replied, "but I can't guarantee an answer."

"What was the result of Tyler's autopsy report?"

"Ah, you want to make sure that you've got your facts straight! We received the report this morning, and there is nothing curious or surprising about the coroner's findings. It is common knowledge, and I presume that you are aware that he was stabbed with a pitchfork."

Huber nodded.

"I see no harm in giving you the essence of the autopsy report." He held out a hand to the sergeant, who provided him with the document.

After briefly looking it over, he said, "Without going into detail, here is the gist of the matter: The summary of the report indicates that there were four puncture wounds in the anterior chest wall. The punctures penetrated deeply into the lungs, causing intrathoracic hemorrhage." He gave the report back to his minion and added, "With damaged lungs and hemorrhage, it is obvious that it didn't take long for him to die."

"Did the pitchfork have four tines?"

"I can see how your mind works. To answer your question, yes, the murder weapon was a four-tine pitchfork."

"Thank you so much," Huber said, and got off the chair.

Chapter 56

"Holy Krewe, you smuggled your piece in!" Andi burst out.

The time was well after two o'clock and the powwow at their favorite spot on the dirt road in full swing.

Huber said, "It was easy! Mrs. White, shaken by the events, was distracted. With Tyler's murder and our getting close to finding out what goes on inside these walls, it can't hurt to be prepared by carrying my pistol. I'll be more than happy if there is no occasion to use it, though." She emphasized, "We *are* close, correct?"

"Yes, boss, I've been doin' lots of thinkin'."

"I'm listening!"

So Andi conveyed her information, starting with Dewayne finding Tyler's body in the tool shed and ending by recounting her confrontation with Mona. The seasoned sleuth paid keen attention to Andi's long account.

Then she asked, "How and when did Dewayne come upon the scene?"

"It was soon after dinner. He was getting the soil ready for planting lettuce in the field yesterday afternoon, and - -"

"I know; I saw him at work and we had a chat."

"Anyhow, during dinner he remembered that he'd left the rake out. The Whiz is strict about always returning tools to the tool shed, so right after the meal Dewayne hurried back to retrieve it. He found Tyler as he was putting the rake into the shed."

"I take it that he was no longer alive and beyond help at that time."

"I asked Dewayne and he told me that he didn't dare touch him, but knew Tyler was dead. He also said that he made sure not to get in contact with the bloody pitchfork that he saw lying near the body."

Huber stated, "That young man is sharp. During our talk he let me know that, in his opinion, Mike was murdered. He seemed to have come to that conclusion even before Tyler's homicide."

"Yeah, Dewayne is street smart and nothing gets by him! And I betcha he's right. Can't believe two deaths in a row are likely to be a coincidence."

"I agree."

"But what was the motive for Mike's murder?"

"According to Tyler, Mike was blackmailing someone. He told me that he'd let me know whom, but sadly the boy didn't live to make good his promise. It is all hearsay at this point, though."

"I can see Mike as a blackmailer," Andi said.

"Now let's go into your impression that there is a link between the young people who don't seem under the Whiz's spell - - as you put it - - and the solving of our mystery. What do you have in mind?"

"I wish I knew!"

"Could it be that the more inquisitive minds are unaffected by the Whiz's charm? Did Tyler belong to the non-influenced group, by the way?"

Andi reflected for a moment and then said, "No, I remember looking at him during the Whiz's pep talk and he appeared to worship the man. So there goes that theory!"

"What is Ratio D?"

"I haven't got a clue, but Tyler mentioned it and I heard about it again later, but can't recall when or where. I'm afraid that I don't pay enough attention to detail and am not a good detective."

"Nonsense. Forgetting how we learned about information happens to the best of us, so don't beat yourself up, Andi."

Then she said, "Tell me about the noises you heard coming from Dr. Morrison's laboratory."

"I'm not sure about that. I was in bad shape at the time and hardly paid attention, but looking back, I think I heard faint whimpering noises."

"Were the sounds animal or human?"

"I don't know; could've been either, and I'm not even positive that I heard them or that they came from the lab."

A flock of birds flew above their heads before landing on a citrus tree nearby, making them momentary intruders to the women's privacy.

Huber laughed and said, "Good thing these creatures can't transmit information!" Then she became serious again and said, "Getting to your face-down with Mona, did she use the exact words, 'We girl campers are doomed'?"

"Sure did."

"'Doomed' is a powerful word! It could mean doomed to die, but I think Mona used it in the sense of having no choice in the matter."

Jacob's statement flashed into Andi's mind and she said, "Like being programmed?"

"Exactly!"

"But Mona said that only the girls were doomed, and from what I caught on in the assembly hall during the Whiz's pep talk and from what Jacob told me, male campers seem to be programmed also."

Huber became grave as she said, "I dread that with the girls the programmer has gone a step further."

"I hope you don't mean what I think you mean!"

"It would explain why Emily has given up."

Andi exclaimed, "Oh, shit!" And then, "Sorry, boss, it slipped out."

"To change the subject, are you still given the Antabuse medication?"

"Uh-huh. Doc gives me the treatment every morning before we start with the therapy session, except today, since the schedules are messed up because of the police investigation. First Doc himself was questioned, followed by the girl campers, and now everyone's therapy appointment is delayed and out of order. My time with him is set for later in the afternoon."

"I am so sorry that I put you through that miserable ordeal; I had no idea that something of that sort was involved when I sent you here."

"That's okay, Mrs. Huber, and all part of the job," she said with a smirk. "And it won't happen again. No matter what, I won't swallow another drop of alcohol while getting the treatment."

"My hotel has Internet access and I looked it up last night. The drug disulfiram will not do you any harm by itself. Knowing that, I feel a little better, but I wish you could have stayed drug free while doing this investigation."

Andi suddenly shouted, "Drug free! That's it!" And tapping her forehead disgustedly, she said, "Should've figured that out a lot sooner."

Before her boss had a chance to inquire what she meant, the redhead had another brainstorm and announced, "Of course, Ratio D! I remember now, I didn't hear about it some more after Tyler mentioned it; I *read* about it.

Chapter 57

By the time Huber and Andi had reached a game plan, it was past three in the afternoon. Together they had mulled over every aspect of the case until they were certain that they had arrived at the truth. They knew now what had prompted both murders. Consequently, they had unmasked the villain. The two agreed that to inform the lieutenant of their findings at this point was useless since their evidence was all circumstantial and they had no concrete proof.

Both concurred that to set a trap for the culprit and provoke him was the way to go. Who should do the provoking and how best to go about it was their only dispute. Huber was uncomfortable with sending her assistant to confront the antagonist without a weapon yet was unwilling to hand over her pistol. Andi, for her part, felt confident that she could handle the assignment unarmed.

She argued, "You've got to admit, boss, that it's more natural for me to do the tackling. No disrespect, but you've already blown your cover."

Huber smiled and said, "Only where Lieutenant Johansson and his sergeant are concerned. The officers know about your position as well. Sorry, but I couldn't avoid it." She added, "I'm sure that the lieutenant realizes that it serves his investigation best if he keeps the knowledge to himself."

"Maybe, but how much longer do you think you can string the Whiz along with the reporter story? It's only a matter of time before he gets wise to it, and then he'll show you the gate. He can't throw me out; I'm a paying customer!"

"You have a point, and I agree that it makes more sense for you, as an insider, to toss the bait. Still, I'm worried. The beast, to use Mona's expression, is extremely cunning and dangerous; remember what happened to Mike and Tyler."

Andi said, "The boys were taken by surprise. I, on the other hand, plan to be on my guard every step of the way."

"Okay, you're on, but only under the condition that you can stage the ultimate showdown outdoors. Do I make myself clear?"

"Sure thing, Mrs. Huber! Reckon I know what's in your head."

And so they worked out some of the details, while deciding that others would best be played by ear.

Chapter 58

At last they parted and went their opposite directions. Andi rode her Harley back toward the main building to freshen up before her session with Doc Morrison, and Huber felt an urge for physical activity, opting to hike around the entire property. She continued on the connecting path until reaching the main dirt road close to the lower wall of the compound. Nothing like a brisk walk to clear the mind, she told herself. And her mind was by no means at ease. So many things could go wrong with the plan they had formed. Andi was full of youthful enthusiasm and indeed capable, but was she truly aware of the enormous danger that lay ahead? The undertaking is out of my hands now, Huber mused; no sense in fretting over it.

The temperature was still in the upper eighties on this late afternoon, and she was perspiring as she trekked up the trail leading around the semi-circle of the property's western end. Moments later, she paused near the foot of the vineyard and looked up at the rows of vines, heavy with nearly ripe grapes. She couldn't help but wondering what would be the fate of these precious fruits come harvest time, should Revamp Camp have to close its doors.

She waved to a group of youngsters digging up the bounty of the earth as she walked alongside the potato field. Approaching the vegetable gardens, she spotted a lonely figure at some distance away. The person was laboring with a spade, upturning patches of earth in an energetic manner. Getting closer, she realized that the man hard at work was none other than the Whiz. He did not seem to notice her and kept at it. Pearls of sweat had formed on his forehead and his ponytail lay damp against his neck as he appeared to grind himself into a frenzy. He finally looked at her but did not utter a word and kept toiling away.

Huber said, "That's an excellent method to get your exercise!"

At last he stopped his labor, leaned on the spade, and between heavy breaths replied, "Might as well work in the field since the lieutenant has taken over my office."

"I am sorry for what has happened."

He did not acknowledge her sentiment and continued, "It was irritating enough to have the Social Services people breathe down my back about Mike, and now the Sheriff is presiding over my business."

"Sorry about that too! Oh, and Mr. White, I'm finished with the interviews. As soon as I know, I'll inform you on which day the article will appear in the paper."

He let out an unhappy snicker and retorted, "No matter what you write about the merits of Revamp Camp won't make any difference now. Who wants to send their kid to a rehab facility where murder is on the agenda?"

She could not argue with that and said, "Well, thank you for your hospitality," and walked on.

Chapter 59

Because of the ongoing police investigation, Doc Morrison had shortened the campers' therapy sessions to twenty minutes or less for this day, since he also had to work around their classroom schedules. Administering treatments took a short amount of time, and only the most recently admitted camper and a handful of others required daily therapy; the rest had theirs every third day. Still, he had an average of fourteen kids requiring counseling on any given day, and he had to be through with them before the dinner horn sounded. Actually, since the tragedies, that number was now down to twelve.

In today's sessions, the focus had predominantly revolved around Tyler's murder. The feelings on the topic among his patients had been shock, disbelief, sadness, fear, anxiety and a certain amount of curiosity. At the moment, Andi's appointment was coming to an end, and, as in previous instances, he was not sure where he stood with her. The young woman was hard to read. When asked how Tyler's death made her feel, she had replied with one word: angry.

Now her twenty minutes were up and the doctor said, "See you tomorrow, Andi."

She did not budge.

"This is all the time we have today."

Again, she stayed put and just glared at him.

Annoyed, he stated, "I have more patients to see, and my wife expects me to come home for dinner tonight!"

"Tyler was my friend."

"I'm sorry. We'll discuss it tomorrow."

"No, sir," she shot back, "we'll discuss it now!"

Surprised at the force of her outburst, he looked at his watch and said, "Okay, if it's that urgent, I'll give you five more minutes."

"Tyler told me all the secrets he'd ferreted out about you."

"What the dickens are you talking about?"

"He knew that Mike was blackmailing you, for one."

"He knew nothing of the sort, and neither do you. Get out of here, you're wasting my time."

Andi calmly went on, "He confided all of what goes on with some of your girl patients."

"You are totally out of line here. Tyler had a wild imagination and no one took him seriously. I certainly paid no attention to his fabrications."

"Maybe so, but in your case he was right on! I've done my own homework."

An alert flicker appeared in Doc's eyes now and he asked, "What is that supposed to mean?"

"Remember when I asked you if you kept rats in your lab? Well, they weren't rats, but the whimpering cry of a girl. Betcha it was Emily."

"Tyler's outrageous tales must have been contagious; you're starting to sound like him."

Andi ignored the remark and continued, "As far as Mike's blackmailing, he wanted a piece of the girl-action, didn't he?"

"You're crazy and have absolutely no proof of these accusations."

"That's where you're wrong. Tyler kept a journal, and he also told me about Ratio D."

There was fear now in his eyes when he demanded, "What do you know about Ratio D?"

"It is a mind-altering drug you concocted in your lab and you use it for controlling campers."

"As I said, Tyler had a wild imagination."

"Oh, but it exists! I found it myself the day I used your computer. At the time, I was just checking my e-mail account, but later recalled seein' it in your document file. The title read: *Ratio D – Formula for mind altering drug.*"

He was nervous now, but kept up the pretense. "That doesn't tell you a thing."

"Sure does! You give this Ratio D drug to the substance abuse kids, telling them that it is a medication to treat their addictions, but the drug actually gives you power over them, and they become wax in your hands. You programmed them to worship the Whiz - - that's why they're hangin' on every word that comes out of his mouth - - and you use and abuse the girls for your own creepy desires."

There was a knock at the door and Brandon stuck his head in, saying, "I'm here for my session."

"Just wait your turn. I'm not finished with Andi here," Doc snapped at him.

He waited until the door closed again and then asked, "Are you through?"

"Not by a long shot. Now where was I?" She pinned him with an accusing stare and went on, "Oh yeah, you used your Ratio D invention to render the girl campers docile, so molesting them was a cinch. I wonder how long you worked on the formula until you came up with the perfect drug for your sick purpose."

She had finally pushed a button, and his words sputtered out in rapid succession, "That's not at all how it happened. I had done research for years, trying to find an effective medication to treat cocaine and crack addiction. When I discovered what I'm calling Ratio D, I thought that I had arrived at last. To my utter amazement, I had created a drug that has an entirely different effect. By the way, I haven't given up on finding an antidote for cocaine; that is still my top priority research."

"But in the meantime you just use your shameless Ratio D formula for your evil doin's."

"Wrong, I'm experimenting with it for the benefit and furtherance of science." He gave a malicious laugh and said, "You guessed right. While under the influence of Ratio D, it is easy to make the patients venerate the Whiz. The man himself is under the impression that he has his campers under total control by the sheer power and charm of his personality."

"And how do you justify molesting the girl campers? Is that also done to benefit science?"

"I have to include all aspects of the drug's capabilities in my study."

"That's bull."

"Give me a break! These girls have all been around the block plenty of times before they were sent here. They are no saintly virgins, for Christ's sake!"

Andi looked at him gravely and stated, "They are minors."

He didn't answer and looked at his watch again.

Andi continued, "When Mike tried to blackmail you, he needed to be eliminated. Since he was diabetic, overdosing him with insulin was easy as pie. His death looked and was accepted as accidental and you thought you were home free. You would've gotten away with it too if it hadn't been for good old Tyler getting wise to you."

There was no pretence of innocence any longer as he barked, "If you wanted what is commonly called justice, you'd have delivered me to the Sheriff by now. So are you giving it a shot at blackmail too?"

"Possibly."

"You can't want a piece of the action - - like you put it - - so what's it going to be?"

"I figure that Ratio D is worth a bundle and I want some of the rights to it."

"Impossible; you've gone mad!"

"Take it or leave it. Lieutenant Johansson is just a few steps down the hallway."

He kept silent for some time, and Andi was conscious of the growing danger. The doctor was obviously contemplating how best to eliminate her. All her senses were suddenly on high alert, and she would have heard a pin drop, had one fallen onto the cushioned carpet. Then the moment was over.

When he spoke again, it was with forced ease, "I'll draw something up later, and I'm sure that we can come to an agreement. I don't want to keep Brandon waiting much longer, so tell me quickly about the journal you mentioned."

"What about it?"

"You can give it to me later when we sign the" - - he cleared his throat - - "rights to the Ratio D agreement. For now, just tell me what he wrote in it."

"I never read it. Didn't have to, as Tyler told me all he knew."

"So just bring me the damned thing later."

"I don't have it, but I know where it's at."

"Where?"

"You'll never find it on your own. Tyler buried it in the fields and showed me the exact spot."

He eyed her keenly and said, "You'd better not be tricking me or I'll guarantee you'll regret it!" And then, "I believe it, though. It would be typical of Tyler to have kept a journal listing everyone's nasty little secrets. I can also picture him burying it, the drama king that he was."

Then he sighed and stated, "I guess you give me no choice. I can't get away until dinnertime. Where do you suggest we meet?"

"Be at the tool shed after the horn toots for supper," she replied and jumped to her feet.

"Wait! Will you be riding your motorcycle to the shed?"

"You got it!"

Andi had already walked down the hallway and out of the building when she asked herself the question, why does it make a difference to him whether I'll show up riding my Harley or on foot?

Chapter 60

Doc Morrison was going through the motions of his last patient's therapy session for the day, but he hardly paid attention to what the kid was telling him. His mind was bent on what lay ahead for him that evening, and he was mulling over a plan of action.

The camper was just warming up to his subject when Doc interrupted with, "We're done for now; you can tell me the rest during your next session."

Dumbfounded, the kid got up and left, and the doctor locked the door behind him. He quickly called his wife to let her know that he was delayed at the camp once more. At least this time he had a good excuse and blamed the ongoing police investigation. Typing up the so-called agreement only took a couple of minutes. Then he opened the door to his lab, entered, and got busy with a bit of preparation.

The doctor timed leaving his office just right, so that he passed the administrative office at the exact moment when the horn for the call to dinner blasted. He waved good-bye to Mrs. White through the open door as she was getting up from her desk in anticipation of the meal, then walked on toward the front entrance. Behind him, he heard the sound of the lady's pumps clip-clapping against the tiled floor as she left her domain and walked down the hallway. Making sure the coast was clear, he retraced his steps, sauntered by her office again, turned down the corridor leading to the opposite wing, and exited via the back door.

Inside, and around the tool shed, members of the Santa Barbara County Sheriff's Department had finished at the scene in the late afternoon, and the crime tape had been removed. The place appeared tranquil and innocent once more.

Doc Morrison was the first to arrive and waited, standing in front of the shed. He could not bring himself to sit down on the bench; the image of Mike perched there, puffing away on his cigarettes, was too real to him. By the same token, he did not allow himself a peek inside the shed. He did not believe in ghosts, but the place felt eerie to him. It was doubtful that the phrase, *The culprit always returns to the scene of the crime*, had any validity. Indeed, he wished he wasn't here.

Outrage welled up in him as he thought, the nerve of Andi! What arrogance of the young woman to demand rights to my Ratio D. I researched and labored for years to arrive at the precious formula, had to eliminate two people who posed a threat to my invention, and now this brazen girl wants a piece of the pie. Rights to my brain-child, outrageous! Why had she suggested that they meet at this exact spot, he wondered. Was that damned journal buried here of all places?

Now he heard the sound of her motorcycle and was about to find out.

Chapter 61

Andi parked her Harley next to the Kubota tractor, got off it, and walked the few yards to where her adversary was waiting.

He said, "Show me where he buried the journal."

"Not so fast! Do we have an agreement?"

"Sure." He opened his briefcase, took out a single sheet of paper, and handed it over.

Andi read the few words: *"I herewith promise to discuss with Antoinette LeJeune the eventuality of turning over some rights to Ratio D with the understanding that she provides me with Tyler's journal in return."*

"That doesn't mean diddly! And it's not dated or signed. Your name's not even on it."

"I didn't have much time to draw up an agreement. We can work out the details later and then date and sign it."

"Perhaps."

"So let's get on with this. Take me to the journal."

"First I have a couple of questions."

He looked around. There wasn't a soul in sight, so he said, "Okay, but make it snappy."

"How did you get Mike to come here to the shed?"

"What do you mean?"

Andi said, "I can understand how you got Tyler to come. After all, he was one of your Ratio D victims, and you could make him do whatever you liked. But what about Mike? He was not under the influence, so how did you get him to agree to meet you here?"

"I don't particularly like you, Andi, but I've got to admit that you're sharp. His reason for blackmailing was to 'get in on the action,' as he put it. I supplied him with a pack of cigarettes and told him to meet me at the shed where I would make good on the rest of the bargain. I didn't specify, but I think he was under the impression that 'the action' would happen in the shed. From what transpired in his therapy sessions, I also knew that he resented being made to give up smoking and felt sure that he would chain-smoke, given the chance. That fact was important to my plan, but I don't want to go into all that now."

Andi said, "The other thing I want to know is also about Mike. What kind of strong evidence did he have against you that prompted his extortion?"

"He caught me in the act. Even though he was not suicidal, the Whiz and I had decided to keep Mike in short insulin supply, which meant that he had to come to me for a refill every few days. I accidentally failed to give it to him during his therapy session one day, and he returned to my office to retrieve it. I was careless that one time and forgot to lock the door, and he saw me with one of the girl patients.

"Now I've answered your questions, so no more delays."

"Fair enough."

Andi made a big show of walking over to the west side of the small shed. Then she took big steps away from it, counting each step out aloud as she went along. After the seventh, she turned 90 degrees and took another three steps in that direction, and then stood still, saying, "This is the spot; get a shovel."

The prospect of going inside the shed was not a pleasant one, but he forced down the disturbing feeling and went to retrieve a shovel. Then he walked to where Andi still stood, keeping one foot on the exact place.

She said, "Start diggin'."

He stared at her incredibly and asked, "You want me to dig?"

"Sure thing, if you care to find the journal."

So for the first time in his life, Doc Morrison applied himself to manual labor and dug. And he dug, and dug, and then dug some more. Thanks to the summer season, it was still light out enough to see.

He had unearthed about half a square yard and was sweating profusely when Andi finally shrugged and stated, "Maybe I'm wrong and the spot is on the north side of the shed."

He threw the shovel down and shouted, "You double-crossing bitch! There is no journal. I've been had."

He marched to the bench where he had left his briefcase, opened it, took out a small object, and dropped it into his trouser pocket. Then he came back to where he had dug the hole in the ground and picked up the shovel again. Andi had watched him silently having no idea what he was up to, but got out of his way as he bent down to pick up the tool.

He suddenly came after her and, raising it, yelled, "Get on your motorcycle and start the engine!"

He left her no choice but to obey. As he closely followed her to the Harley, waving the shovel above her head in a threatening fashion, every inch of her body and mind was on maximum alert.

Once she was straddled on the bike and had hit the starter button, he dropped the gardening tool and in a swift motion reached inside his pocket and grabbed the syringe.

While pulling off the safety cap, he hissed, "You're going for a ride, losing control, and having an accident."

He was about to push on the plunger, when he heard a commanding voice holler, "Hold it right there!"

Doc swirled around to face Huber, who had stepped out from behind the cover of the shed. He stopped with his arm in mid-air, paralyzed for a second.

Huber aimed her pistol directly at his heart and ordered, "Drop the syringe!"

He was recovering from the initial shock and ridiculed, "You wouldn't have the guts to pull the trigger!"

"Try me," Huber shot back.

Andi seized the moment, and, swinging one leg off the bike, kicked the syringe out of his hand with the heel of her boot, making the instrument fall to the ground. Huber was already closing in on him, holding her weapon steadily with both hands.

Without altering her aim, and never taking her eyes off the doctor, she said, "Good job Andi! Now ride off to get help; I think the Sheriff is still around. I'm staying put and making sure that Doc Morrison doesn't get any ideas of trying to escape or pick up his syringe."

Chapter 62

One glorious day in October, Peter and Regula Huber stood on top of a mountain called Montjuic that overlooked the city of Barcelona, Spain, to one side and the ocean on the other. Perched on the summit's cliff was the Montjuic castle. They stood in the fortress's courtyard and admired the spectacular view. There were two ocean cruisers docked in the harbor and they watched a third making its way in. Although sunny with a temperature of 67 degrees Fahrenheit, it was extremely windy at the peak, and Peter had to hold on tight to his hat while they were exploring the grounds.

To arrive at Montjuic, they had first taken the funicular which was part of the Barcelona subway system, and at the end station transferred to the gondola called Telefèric. On the ride up, the entire city lay at their feet in a breathtaking panorama.

While sitting in the gondola, taking it all in, Regula leaned against her husband's shoulder and said, "This is heaven, but I feel a bit guilty."

"You're thinking about Andi, right?"

She nodded. "Thank God it's all behind her now. She called me this morning while you were exploring the town doing research for your book. It was nine in the morning here and midnight of the previous day her time."

"So the trial is over?"

"Yes, it came to an end yesterday, but she waited with the phone call, making sure we would be up. Doc Morrison was convicted of child molestation, murder in the first degree of Mike and Tyler, and the attempted murder of Andi. He got a life sentence without parole."

"I can imagine the verdict was a result of Andi's testimony."

"Correct where the murders are concerned, but it was Mona and Tracy's testimony that nailed him for the molestation charge."

Peter said, "I don't understand why the girls didn't come forward while it was going on. Surely they could have talked to the Whiz."

"It's complicated, and Andi told me that all came out during the trial. Doc's Ratio D drug was apparently addictive. Not only was it mind altering, but it also made them feel good. They needed their daily fix as it gave them the illusion that their lives would be over without it."

"Good Lord! That sounds like science fiction."

"Coming back to Mona and Tracy, they knew deep down that what they were doing was wrong but could not help the craving for the drug and consequently what Doc Morrison made them do while they were under the influence of it. They hated the man with a passion but were helpless and totally in his power. Their imaginary 'killing of the beast' was their emotional defense and kept them sane. Mona, of course, was the stronger of the two, and I think that she instigated the 'night talks' for her friend's protection."

Regula sighed and continued, "Emily was not that lucky. The girl lacked the emotional stamina and became detached. It was revealed in the trial that the doctor realized Emily could not handle the drug and took her off it. The girl then begged him for it since she was highly addicted, but he refused. So the whimpering that Andi, and probably also Tyler, heard coming from Doc's laboratory was the agonizing outcries when she was going through withdrawal. The doctor actually said that she was his only failure in the experiment. Can you believe the gall of the man?"

"Did Emily testify?"

"No. According to Andi, she was in no shape to be put on the stand and was spared the agony."

"I'll call Roger soon to see how she's doing."

The gondola had taken them about halfway up when Regula pointed below and said, "Look, some people are hiking up on the trail. Guess we could've done that."

"That would've taken all day! Coming back to what we were discussing, I never understood what role the cigarettes played in Mike's murder. Isn't it a fact that he died from an overdose of insulin?"

"That was made clear in court too. Doc covered himself twice, so to speak. He gave him the pack of cigarettes initially as a sort of bonus for holding his tongue while waiting for the real blackmail pay-off. He knew the kid well enough to predict that he'd smoke the pack rapidly. He had planned to inject him with an overdose of insulin from the start, but then also came up with the idea of making it look like nicotine poisoning, just to be misleading. So when he met Mike outside the shed that evening, he was equipped with both, a syringe full of insulin and a nicotine patch."

"I still don't get it. What exactly did he do?"

"The way I picture it - - and it may have been done differently - - is this: He walks up to Mike, who is puffing away, saying something like, 'Sorry I'm late, but I brought you something.' Reaching into his pocket, he remarks, 'Watch out, you dropped a glowing ash between your legs.' While Mike is busy looking at his crotch, Doc gets the syringe ready in a flash and injects him with a massive dose of insulin into the thigh."

Peter chuckled and said, "You've got some imagination!"

She continued, "Of course, Mike knew better than to leave the nicotine patch on while smoking, so Doc waited until he was comatose and then put the patch he had brought with him on Mike's arm."

"I get the picture now!"

Then he asked, "Did you suspect Doc Morrison to be the criminal from the start?"

"Not at all," his spouse replied. "Before the murders, Andi had tagged Mike as being the bad guy. And later we both were suspicious of the Whiz, thinking that he must be using drugs to keep his campers under his spell. Then when Andi suddenly connected the dots as far as the drug-free campers were concerned, and also remembered that she came across a Ratio D document on Doc's computer, we realized that we had the right idea but the wrong person."

"I don't get the 'drug-free camper' thing."

"Let me explain. Andi had observed all along that some of the young people were not influenced by the Whiz but had not figured out why that was. Then, when she had that brainstorm, it became clear that the common factor was that these campers had not been drug abusers before coming to Revamp Camp. Naturally, the abusers were treated with medication by Doc Morrison. He couldn't very well inject the kids who were not substance abusers with a treatment."

"That makes sense."

"Doc being the villain also explains why so many of the campers were lethargic, acting like zombies on weekends. Since he was not there to administer the Ratio D drug, they were going through withdrawal symptoms, especially on Sundays. They did not know of their addiction, thinking that they were getting treatments."

He asked, "Was there mention in the trial what the doctor had planned to inject Andi with, when you ambushed him?"

"Oh, yes, I forgot to tell you. They found a large dose of Methadone in the syringe."

"But that's used for heroin addicts. I didn't know it was lethal."

"Anything can be lethal if overdone, but the Methadone was not meant to kill her. Had he succeeded with injecting her, she would have become drowsy and lost consciousness. The idea was for her to lose control over her bike and have an accident. Remember, he forced her onto it."

Peter shook his head and said, "I can't believe all this from a physician. He is supposed to heal and comfort; the guy took the Hippocratic oath, for crying out loud!"

"I'm sure that was his initial intention when he first practiced medicine at Revamp Camp, but then he got carried away with his research and invention. I think that he considers himself primarily a scientist, and practicing medicine seems secondary to him. Andi said that when taking the stand, he insisted that his experimental discoveries and procedures with Ratio D were done for the furtherance of science and would benefit future generations."

"Never mind that he shamefully used human beings as guinea pigs. The scumbag has a family, right?"

"A wife and two kids. I would assume that they'll move out of state and change their name."

"Out of the country might be even better."

Then Regula remarked, "I'm sure glad Andi posed as an alcohol abuser and not as a drug addict, or she'd have been given Ratio D." She shivered, "I would have never forgiven myself!"

Peter said, "Let's think about something more pleasant where Andi is concerned. I'm glad she took us up on the offer to stay in our guest bedroom while attending UCLA. It's not exactly next door to the college, but closer than Pasadena."

"She's a breath of fresh air to have around!"

At that point they had arrived at the summit of Montjuic and applied themselves to some serious sight-seeing.

A week later, Huber called Andi from Zurich, Switzerland:

"Hi there, Mrs. Huber, are ya'll having a good time?"

"We would have, except for the weather. It has been raining ever since we got here, and according to the forecast, we have another storm system coming our way. I have a good mind to chuck it all and come home early."

"Holy Krewe! I'd best get busy cleaning up the mess in your house from all the raisin' hell and partyin' that's been going on 'round here."

For a split second Huber was alarmed, and then she laughed out loud.

EPILOGUE

The following are points of interest concerning the future of Revamp Camp staff members and campers:

James White: Despite the hardship after the tragedies, the Whiz overcame his obstacles and kept Revamp Camp alive by pure perseverance and willpower.

Doreen White: Divorced the Whiz and eventually adopted a baby. Whether she remarried or raised the child by herself is unknown.

Heather Sotto: Stayed on at the facility and became the Whiz's right hand as his most trusted employee.

Kyle Norton and **Roberta Ralston:** The sports coach and the teacher tied the knot and continued their work at Revamp Camp.

Bob Gilmore: Took a teaching position in New Zealand.

Mona: Opened a novelty store in Solvang where she sold her exquisite dollhouse creations, made possible with the financial backing of her mom.

Tracy: Went to work for Mona as a salesclerk.

Brandon: Finished high school at Revamp Camp, went on to college, and ultimately became a responsible adult.

Dewayne: Entered a reality show dance competition with his Hip Hop routine and won first prize, making him an overnight celebrity.

Jacob: The Whiz hired him as music teacher at Revamp Camp.

Emily: Did not trust a soul, not even her parents, for a long time to come. It took years before she fully recovered.

Doc Morrison: Spent the rest of his life behind bars, showing no remorse whatsoever. It is rumored that he tried to negotiate a deal to sell his Ratio D – Formula to the Pentagon, but that's another story.

R. A. Huber Mysteries by Alice Zogg

Revamp Camp
Final Stop Albuquerque
The Fall of Optimum House
The Lonesome Autocrat
Tracking Backward
Turn the Joker Around
Reaching Checkmate

Available at www.amazon.com,
www.barnesandnoble.com
and other vendors.